C

FURY

ON THE

PLAINS

Center Point
Large Print

This Large Print Book carries the Seal of Approval of N.A.V.H.

CHAD MERRIMAN

FURY

ON THE

PLAINS

CENTER POINT PUBLISHING

THORNDIKE, MAINE

This Center Point Large Print edition
is published in the year 2003 by arrangement with
Golden West Literary Agency.

The text of this Large Print edition is unabridged. In other
aspects, this book may vary from the original edition. Printed in
Thailand. Set in 16-point Times New Roman type by
Bill Coskrey and Gary Socquet.

ISBN 1-58547-306-5

Library of Congress Cataloging-in-Publication Data.

Merriman, Chad.
  Fury on the plains / Chad Merriman.--Center Point large print ed.
    p. cm.
  ISBN 1-58547-306-5 (lib. bdg. : alk. paper)
  1. Large type books. I. Title.

PS3553.H38 F8 2003
813'.54--dc21

                                                        2002041278

CHAPTER ONE

H E came on the camp, where a splinter of meadowland lay beside the Hell Gate trail, just as the sun broke over and began to settle toward the green of the lowering mountains. He could smell the pine in the close-hugging timber and hear the sibilance of needles whose sound was that of the gentlest rain.

But he neither watched nor listened to what lay about him at the moment; that had scarcely changed all day. His eyes were fixed on something odd and surprising on the trail ahead of his horse. It was calico, dyed red and yellow, with a frilled hem and long cloth ties that made it the kitchen apron of some woman. It was so fresh that it must have been dropped within the past few hours.

His name was Ames, Kelsey Ames from Butte. He stood six-two with his boots off, whip-slim and whip-tough. Weather had burned him the brown of the great hill rising above the mining town. The sun had bleached his shirt to a lifeless gray that showed darkness where a year ago the proud patches of a sergeant's chevrons had been. His face was rugged, mobile, quick to warm, and swifter to freeze. A flat-brimmed hat, then and now, was tugged over hair black and feathered, a cavalry hat peaked up to conform to his present and previous trade of punching.

He was tired, and so were his saddle horse and the pack pony that had ambled up to halt behind him. He looked at the apron, then glanced off across the narrow meadow. There was tall grass to conceal its floor, but the grass was bent and trampled.

Somebody had camped on the meadow the night before, although no people or animals were now in evidence. It beat him how a woman would lose a thing like an apron out here on the wilderness trail. He figured he might as well take a look at the campsite.

And thus he found it. He came first to a mountain runnel on the back side of the flat. The camp was still pitched there, detectable down the creek from where he came in to the little stream. But first he saw the man lying face down at a place where obviously three or four horses had been picketed for the night. The horses were gone, and the man lay where a tiny mound of fresh dirt suggested the recent presence of a picket pin. It looked as if the man had just pulled the pin to fetch his horses in to camp to pack up. Then he had been shot, dropped dead in his tracks, the bullet tearing through the side of his gray head and apparently coming from close range.

For the horses, maybe. The outlaw breeds had cross-hatched these mountains with their private runs. But that did not explain the apron, and he felt something very cold deep within himself.

He received a second, smaller shock of surprise when he saw, with a wooden aparejo, two leather saddles. The presence of the saddles seemed to eliminate horse thieves, who would have prized them. The mountain breeze, he noted, had lacked time to weather the char and ash of the campfire, over which a breakfast must have been cooked.

And then, beyond the camp, he saw what accounted in part for the apron. A gleaming bit of flesh rose into view, flesh pointed up in bare breasts, then all of it showing as he stiffened his legs to rise numbly on the stirrup leathers. Without irreverence, he emitted a gusty curse, for then he saw the whole naked, obscene posture of the body that, unlike the man's, had been scalped.

The rest of the hair was yellow, and he saw that she had been a girl in her late teens and had died between attack and scalping from a stab wound under the left breast. Her clothing, ripped to pieces, lay about. Eyes watched the sky without movement, without life. Before he realized his purpose, he had swung down, caught up a saddle blanket, and covered her.

Afterward he stood trembling, having grasped the facts but with the emotional impact still a numb thing that tightened the flesh between his shoulders and tied a knot in his throat. Indian work was never pretty, although he had never directly seen it carried to this extent. But it happened. A man heard about it sometimes with revulsion and fury but without this awful awareness of its reality.

He went back to the dead fire, his eyes brooding about the site. Breakfast had been serene enough, and the camp seemed to have been jumped with carefully planned surprise. The man, out to bring in the horses for another day's travel, had been killed instantly. The girl had run a few steps before she had been caught.

It was plain enough what had happened here. It had

not come out of any desire for robbery or murder or rape. Hate had been at the bottom of this. Indian trouble was brewing in the Idaho settlements, on ahead of him. He would have to go out of his way, past Fort Lapwai, where he could report this thing to the military.

He did not want to bury the dead or disturb the scene much until the Army had sent out a detachment to investigate the facts for yet another unpleasant entry in the record. Nor did he care to leave the bodies exposed to timber wolves and bear. So he went out and brought in the man and put him down beside the girl. He got the tarp off their pack and used that and the other saddle blankets to cover them better. Then he piled the rest of the camp gear on top. He didn't want to search through the personal things after a name. That also was the Army's job. He'd had enough of that when he'd done a hitch in the cavalry. He was all too anxious to swing aboard and put the camp behind him. The circumstances giving rise to his own business in Idaho had made it hit him harder than it might have otherwise.

He hadn't been much impressed by what Trace Buckmaster had said to him two days ago in Butte. In one part of the country or another, it seemed like, there was always some kind of Indian scare. But now, as he rode away from the silent mountain camp, that whole business with Trace came back to him clearly.

He had been belligerent and wary even before he went in to see Trace in his office at the Buckmaster freightyard in Butte. Buckmaster's freight headquarters were like a stockade running beside the dusty side street. A man had emerged through the open gate as Kelsey went toward it. The fellow was burly, with a week's growth of whiskers coiled on a surly face. The marks of his profession were on his loose clothing— sweat and dust and soaked-up axle grease.

"Trace in there, Mack?" Kelsey had said.

"Didn't you hear him chew out my seat just now?"

"Just got to town. What's stuck in his craw this trip?"

The mule skinner peeled sour lips away from brown teeth. "For the most part, Trace just likes the taste of a human bottom. Also, he's sore about you getting here this evening when you were supposed to get here this morning. He asked me if you were on a drunk. Go on in—he'll tell you all about it."

"I reckon."

Walking on through the gateway, Kelsey took the turn to his left. A lean-to tacked to the side of the long, high barn was the office of the largest freighting outfit in Montana. Its door was open, and he walked on in. The acid of hostility openly bit him. Any man who got him to jump through a hoop could put it down as a good day's business.

The room he entered was drab. There was a potbelly stove stained by ill-aimed tobacco juice. The frowning face beyond the desk was supported by the huge figure of a man. A rumble came out of the man. Maybe it was a greeting, maybe it was a belch.

"Sent word you were to be here bright and early for a special job."

"That's right, Trace. And sent me an extra job by the same man who brought me the message. Them galled horses. Took time to doctor them. Look, Trace. We were heading for a showdown when Glenna went away. She went thinking a little separation would be good for all of us. It's only been worse with her gone, and you and me might as well have it out."

"Some other time," Trace had said. "She wants to come home hell ahiking, and that's why I sent for you."

"Why didn't you say so?"

"When I send for a man I don't figure on having to convince him I've got a good reason. You're going over to Mount Idaho and get her. Then you're coming back by way of Lewiston to pick up some horses I ordered from Tooney Bishop."

"What got into Glenna? She figured on staying another month."

"You ain't heard talk about the Indian trouble?"

"Nothing that worried me," Kelsey said.

"Well, me neither," Trace said, "till I got her letter yesterday. They got about the last batch of nonreservation Indians in the country over there. The Army don't like it and got foolish. Laid down a thirty-day deadline. Time's about up, the settlers are scared, and Glenna wants to come home quick." The shirt-sleeved, unshaven man who was as rich as any man in mining-rich Butte laced his fingers behind his head, staring past Kelsey thoughtfully. "I got a letter from Lafe Halverson in the same mail. His scared me worse than Glenna's. He thinks trouble's coming himself, and

Lafe don't go off half-cocked. You can take a message and save me answering his letter. Just tell him I'm ready to do business at the old stand if he's right about what's coming."

"I start now?"

"Blast you, you should have started this morning. And another thing. You and Glenna have got to get it decided between you. I hate dilly-dallying. I think you're scared of her."

"Am I scared of you?"

Trace grinned finally, as if it hurt, but it was really pride that brought it on. "Well, they do say she's a chip off the old block. But in skirts, which can be a hell of a lot more dangerous."

"We see alike there."

"Well, I—I hoped all winter there'd be wedding bells in June. The month's about over. You two got to get it settled."

"Not till she changes her mind about me marrying you and your business along with her."

"Goddamn you, Kelsey, I ought to have fired you six months ago."

"Why didn't you?"

"Because, damn my eyes, I sort of like the cut of you."

So now Kelsey Ames had a cold fear eating like lye at his inwards. Glenna Buckmaster was at Slate Creek, and even if she had already come in to Mount Idaho to meet him, she was still in the middle of the territory so implacably claimed by the nontreaty Nez Percés. He kept thinking that the dead girl had shared much with

11

Glenna, youth and beauty and maybe love in her heart for some man. He kept thinking—hell, how could a man help it?—that somebody might be finding Glenna as he had found the one now back along the trail.

Night had come on, and the timber about had thinned to let him emerge under a clear, star-pointed sky. White pine gave way to the sage that crept into every open plateau. The land smoothed to a great mesa, with only thin fingers of the feathery forest running forward on either hand. Soon starlight showed him a huddle of distant log buildings that was his destination.

It was only a trading post fallen into disuse. When he came within earshot, he let out a hail. Trees rose thinly over the place, whose windows showed him no light. He was all but there when the abrupt drum of horses struck his ears. They ran away from him, on the blind side of the old trading post. He reined in, quickly lifting his carbine out of the saddle boot. With it clutched across his chest, he spurred forward.

Starshine soon showed him the half-naked bodies of three or four Indians, riding west and fanning their ponies. Rage burst in him, carrying the impetus of what he had seen and felt at that desolate camp of the dead back up the trail. In the short while he had been there, he now realized, a change had occurred in him, rendering the trouble on this side of the Bitterroots an immediate, cogent, terribly personal thing to him at this moment. He bit off a bitter curse as he flogged his horse across the lowering sageland, resolved to exact something of retribution from the fleeing savages.

They kept out of range, and long ago he had learned the futility of mere noisy shooting, which might frighten but could not kill. He wanted to kill and kill cruelly, as these creatures had. They ran down over a sharp drop in the broad decline, and he came down over it at a breakneck pound. Afterward it seemed to him that he gained on them a little. Presently he tried a shot, the punch of the exploding powder running out across the land. A muter report forward and a flash of fire told him of a quick and hot retort.

Again and again he asked his horse for more speed, but it had reached its limit. But again he had the sense of closing the gap a little. When they realized it, they would whirl to make their stand. He did not care that the odds were against him. He could see the clear image of a dead girl, a girl with yellow hair. He was seeing his own girl, whom he would fight a whole tribe to protect.

He shot again, then again, and that time drew a volley. But the bullets passed harmlessly by him or fell short of their mark. It was evident to him now that he was drawing within range, it was apparent to the Indians. Then they surprised him completely by splitting in two, two horses cutting to the right, two others bending sharply left. He slackened speed instantly, keenly aware of their cunning.

If he pursued one pair, he would have the other coming in on his back. His mouth sagged open. In one simple maneuver, they had outwitted him, giving him a choice between beating a hasty retreat or going straight forward as hard as he could travel, with them abruptly not the pursued but pursuing. The impulses that so often could drive him had sent him into a deadly trap.

He knew that his best refuge would be Johnny Hite's fort, now far behind him. He swung his horse about but the Indians still rode on away from him, their shapes all but dissolved in the starlit night, the hoofbeats of their streaking ponies rapidly fading. Again surprise jolted through him.

They seemed bent on nothing but making good their own escape. He slackened speed, wanting to see if there was not more than that to it. But on either hand the Indians were well away from him by then and still going. They apparently had not wanted any kind of encounter, even while knowing how greatly they outnumbered him, and that was odd indeed, considering their work up at the dead camp.

As Kelsey grew aware of this release from peril, reaction set him trembling. He realized then what a foolishly dangerous thing he had done, and that he had been saved by the Indians' will and not by his own devices. That was his trouble. Under the right impetus, he could be sudden and headlong, and that was a trait that could shorten a man's life considerably.

Kelsey picked up his pack horse where he had let go of its lead rope and returned to Hite's fort. Its main building was still dark as he rode up to it and yelled, "Johnny! Everything all right here?"

"Who is it?" The voice that came out of the building was Johnny's own and it carried concern.

"Kelsey Ames, from Butte. How's chances to put up

for the night?"

A bull of a man appeared in the doorway. Moonlight showed Kelsey a shaggy, bearded head, shoulders tight in buckskin, and thick legs jammed down woolen pants into leather boots. Johnny Hite came off the post porch, an angry-looking figure.

"That you went skallyhooting past here and done the shooting?" he demanded. "Who the hell do you think you are, man?"

"Now, take it easy," Kelsey retorted just as hotly. "If those weren't redskins on the prowl, I've never seen any."

"They were Nez Percé and friends of mine."

"Well," Kelsey said, "you'd ought to know that there's a dead old man and a dead young girl half a day's travel up the trail. The girl was stripped, raped, and scalped. So when I flushed redskins here, I done some chasing, and I'd do it again."

"What's that you say?" Johnny's voice had a sudden, pinched-up dismay.

Kelsey explained it, sparing none of the details. He watched Johnny's dismay turn into a kind of all-gone despair. Afterward the trader was silent for a long moment.

"Well, I know who the two were," he said then. "Old Lehi Golden and his girl. I think he called her Josie. They come past here around noon yesterday. But you're dead wrong, son, about who done it. No Nez Percé, treaty or nontreaty, ever pulled a stunt like that. Even now, with the nontreaties boiling over, they'd be too smart to pull it. Not when the Army's got a gun against their heads already."

"But who else would, Johnny?"

"Some white renegade scalped that girl after he'd had his fun. To make it look like Injun work. Maybe he had other reasons to make it look that way. You think redskins are the only ones who ever lift a scalp, bub? And Injun's don't have to jump any woman they get a chance at. They got their own. That settles it, to my mind."

"All right," Kelsey said. "I forgot that you spent most of your life among the Nez Percés. Do I get a meal and a bed?"

"Put up your hosses while I set out the grub. Where you heading?"

"Mount Idaho. Got to pick up Trace's girl. She's been visiting on Slate Creek and she's scared."

"She's got reason. If the goddamn Army had used sense, the situation would never have reached this stage. Go on, now, and take care of them cayuses."

Kelsey rode on to a corral that squared off from an old pole barn. He stopped momentarily at the water trough, then turned the horses into the corral, which offered a manger of wild hay. He got a start when he swung back toward the old post building. Lamplight showed in a window on the near side. At the moment he came about, the shadow of what clearly was a woman's body stood painted on the glass. It vanished as he started for the back entrance to the fort.

When he came into the inner quarters, the old trader was alone and putting food on the table. Yet one of the off rooms had a shut door. With the thick smells of age in the main space there was a more subtle one, that of a woman's perfume. Kelsey checked a grin and said nothing about the shadow he had seen. Johnny was no squaw man, but many of the old-timers turned to Indian women when they had need. He figured Johnny had that kind of company and wanted to keep it out of sight.

Turning about, Johnny said, "Look here. Report what you found to the Army, but don't spread it among the settlers any more than you can help. I know them's Army duds you're wearing, and you've likely got the Army's mule head. But no Nez Percé killed Lehi Golden so he could jump Josie. You tell around that one did, there'll be some hanging, and then God knows what."

"I aimed to report it at the fort, and that's all."

"Then you've got sense. Them were nontreaties that you flushed, but they ain't been east of here. I'll vouch for that. And they're taking pains to step wide of trouble right now. At least the ones in these parts. We got the reservation below here, and what nontreaties live south of the reservation are still against going to war. The hotheads are all way over west, on a lake close to Cottonwood. It couldn't even of been some crazy stray that jumped Josie. No Injun goes that far into the mountains except when they all cross to hunt buffalo on the prairie."

"I'm not arguing, Johnny. It looked like Indian work, and that's all I said."

"Just the same, it sizzles my liver the way they get blamed for every piece of dirty work that's pulled hereabouts. Me, I've known whites around here I'd blame first. They come and go all the time. Have ever since the mines brought 'em in here. White scum."

"All right. Can I eat now?"

"Pitch in."

The meal was beans, venison, biscuits, and coffee. Kelsey sat and ate hungrily while the grumpy old trader sucked on his pipe.

"That apron bothers me," Johnny said. "If you hadn't seen it, plain as a rattler wound up on the trail, you'd never have turned off to the camp, would you? And that scalp. Yellow hair and long. There's where they might have slipped. Should have peeled old Lehi's hair just to carry the thing on out."

"Johnny, I wondered about that back there. It looked as if somebody might have planted the apron to make sure the next passer-by went in and found the girl with her scalp gone. Why? If it had been white scum, looks like they'd rather keep it hidden."

"Right now," Johnny answered, "an Injun outrage would sure as hell start a war. Nothing could hold it off." Then, noticing that Kelsey was through eating, he said, "You want to top that off with a piece of pie?"

"When did you start baking pie?"

"Well, I reckon I got company. She scared out when she heard you yell."

"I'll have a piece of her pie," Kelsey said.

CHAPTER TWO

THE pie was first-rate, made from wild berries, and Johnny's mysterious cook was very much in evidence when Kelsey came down from the loft where he had slept. He came to a stop on the steps to look across a room smoky blue with breakfast cooking and heavy with breakfast smells. He had expected to see a squaw left behind by the fleeing Indians. This was a white woman—a slim, fine-featured girl. She had carried a platter of flapjacks to the table and, turning toward him, she met his frank interest with an easy nod.

She was dressed simply yet attractively in a blouse and skirt. Sable-black hair was twisted in a bun at the back of a shapely head. Her body was supple, its lines whispering to him through the soft cloth. But it was her face that held him. It showed an odd quality too deep for his powers of analysis, with brown eyes above high cheekbones and coppery skin.

"Good morning," she said, when he failed to speak. Her voice had a rich vitality, an almost lazy inflection.

"Excuse me," he said. "But you knocked me speechless."

"She's going to keep you company to Mount Idaho, if you don't mind," Johnny Hite said from the kitchen doorway.

"Mind? Do you think I'm crazy?"

"You'd better introduce us, Uncle Johnny," the girl said.

"I forgot. I told her all about you, Ames. She's my niece, sort of. Her daddy and me were partners, back in the old days. Mick Shannon. Her name's Teal."

"I'll be jiggered. I never knew you had a niece, let alone so pretty a one."

"She's been away to school for a long while."

"But," Kelsey said, for the first time remembering that his own plans had been thrown out of kilter, "I've got to go around by the fort. It's a long spell out of the way."

"I don't mind," Teal Shannon said. "I've been cooped up a long while. I want a lot of riding."

"And I want breakfast," Johnny said. "Come on, Ames, and pitch into it."

When the meal was finished, Teal disappeared into her room to pack up. Johnny went out to the barn with Kelsey to saddle a horse for her. Kelsey was privately reflecting on the considerable pleasure that had come into the day's prospect. It was odd, when he was going to fetch home the girl he loved and, if it worked out right, to marry her. It was a weakness that he disliked, a restlessness that perplexed him.

Johnny saddled a nice black for Teal, and they were leading the animals out to the road when the old man swung his glance down the trail to the west, frowning. His own ears seemed to be less keen, for Kelsey had to turn and look before he was aware of an oncoming party of horsemen in the distance.

"By God," Johnny said. "Maybe you're going to be saved the trip to Lapwai. Them's soldiers."

They came on, a squad of cavalry under a corporal.

A tall man with a drooping mustache, the corporal might have ridden on past had not Kelsey held up his hand to flag them down.

Thinking they were bound for Fort Missoula, beyond the mountains, Kelsey said, "Look, Corporal, I come over the hump yesterday, myself. Half a day from here, start looking for a woman's apron on the trail. When you come to it, turn into the camp you'll find on a little creek. But you won't like what I covered up there."

The corporal's eyes had narrowed and, listening, he gave Kelsey a sharp study. "A woman?"

"Yeah. And a man."

"Her hair yellow, kind of?"

"That's right. That what brought you?"

"Yeah. A couple of bucks were caught down the country yesterday evening. They had three horses with a white man's brand, and one of 'em had a scalp hidden in his private junk. The hair was long and corn-colored."

"Well, there you are, Johnny," Kelsey said. "I guess that proves I was right in the first place."

"Army catch 'em?" Johnny asked the corporal.

The noncom shook his head. "Riskin brothers. The bucks put up a fight and got killed. The Riskins brought 'em on to the fort to report it. From the setup, it looked like the bloodthirsty devils had been horsing around up here. But I didn't expect to get any information out of you, old-timer. You're helping those people, and you better watch your step."

Temper swirled up in Johnny Hite, and his shoulders

bunched. Then he shrugged and said, "Go on about your business. There's no use telling you the Riskin boys are as crooked as a dog's hind leg. They've pulled a lot of dirty, sneaking stunts. If they killed some bucks, I allow they 'bushed up to do it, and it weren't in any fight."

"All right, Pop. Don't get exercised." The corporal nodded to Kelsey and rode on, his squad following.

"So you still think I was wrong?" Kelsey said.

"Minute he mentioned the Riskins, I knowed it. But there's no use arguing. You've got a long piece to go today, even without the extra riding. You'd best get started."

Teal had not overheard the conversation, and as far as Kelsey knew, Johnny had spared her the unpleasant news about the dead girl far up on the mountain trail. He was glad of that and wanted to put it out of his own mind, now that he had discharged his responsibility.

He was surprised at the smooth way Teal rose to the saddle and stuck there manwise afterward. She lacked a woman's usual cumbersome equipage, carrying only a saddle roll. With a split skirt and riding boots she wore a woolen sweater and knit cap. He saw that the trip exhilarated her, and also that she kept eying him in some kind of private speculation.

Below Johnny's trading post the forecountry fell away rapidly. It disclosed the blue-hazed canyon of the Clearwater to the south, with a broadening valley downstream and stern brown hills beyond that vanished into purple obscurity.

Kelsey had made the northward swing to Lewiston a

number of times, but now they were turning south into country unfamiliar to him. He was a little uneasy about having Teal under his wing, but he was not going to be caught off guard as Lehi Golden had been.

Once they were down upon the river, the Indian reservation lay directly across from them. But it was occupied, he remembered, by what were called the treaty Indians, that part of the Nez Percé nation that had resigned itself to its fate. The danger to himself and Teal would mount as they got into more distant country. That was where the nontreaties ran, growing ever more hostile, according to the talk.

At last, when Teal showed no inclination to start a conversation, Kelsey said, "You going to live in Mount Idaho?"

She shook her head. "I'm going to visit some relatives near there. After that, I don't know what I'll do."

"Where did you go to school?"

"In Oregon, in an academy, and I hated it. I can't stand being cooped up."

"That's my trouble, too," Kelsey said. "And it's hard to get out of, isn't it?"

She gave him a puzzled glance. "That's odd. I couldn't help overhearing you and Uncle Johnny talk last night. There was something about your being in the Army. I'd say that was the worst kind of regimentation. What drew you to it, then?"

"Maybe I just wanted to be an Injun fighter. I was a kid and looking for excitement. Only did one hitch— with the Seventh, at Fort Lincoln."

"Custer's regiment?"

"That's right. I was in on his finish, but under Reno. I come through."

"And you liked Indian fighting?" she asked.

"No. I only said that might have drawn me into the outfit, thinking it would be exciting and fun. It's exciting enough, but believe me, it's far from fun."

"I'm glad you found out that much, at least. What do you do now?"

"Well," Kelsey said, "the man I work for runs freight wagons and pack strings out of Butte. He's got main lines to Corrine and up to Benton. Then he's got swingers into the Big Hole and over to Bozeman. The outfit uses up horses pretty fast, and there's a ranch where they're rested up and doctored. I run that, with a couple of riders that work for me. Trace Buckmaster's got bigger plans for me. Wants me to come more into the company and work up in it. I don't want to because I want to run a horse ranch of my own. That's why I said we have something in common, not wanting to be cooped up."

"Any reason why you shouldn't quit the man?"

He glanced at her sharply, wondering if Johnny had told her he was over here to meet a girl and take her home. Vaguely he said, "I reckon that's part of the trouble. A man gets attached to things he don't want to break away from unless he's forced to."

"I bet she's pretty," Teal said.

The country had a southward rise toward the primitive area of the Salmon Mountains. They nooned past Kamiah and afterward Teal began to show a close and uneasy preoccupation with the country about them. He felt no great worry, himself. His Army training had given him considerable confidence in his ability to take care of himself. He had a carbine and pistol and knew how to use both expertly. Just the same, he liked less and less the way she kept watching the skylines of the naked brown hills.

At last he said, "What's the matter?"

"I don't know. But I've got a feeling we'd be smart to lose ourselves from here on."

"What does that come from? A woman's intuition?"

"Sorry," she said. "I'm not trying to be bossy. Where you go, I go. The trouble is, my people might not be your people just now."

"What does that mean?"

"Lead on, Sergeant, and I'll follow."

They continued on up a long, narrow valley outskirted by green timber, beyond which ran hazy brown hills. From his sketchy knowledge of the country, Kelsey was sure that the Indian reservation had fallen behind them. Below that, a vast prairie upland swung west from here to the far-off Snake. It was the disputed country, and he began to catch some of the uneasiness still evident in Teal.

Finally he said, "What's chasing us, Irish? Something's sanding your nerves."

"No need for it to worry us both."

"What is it?"

"Stubbornness, maybe. I still don't think we're smart sticking to this well-known trail. Too easy for somebody to 'bush up."

"Indians?"

"My friend, they are no more dangerous than the gentry that dares to call itself white."

He gave her a look of suspicion. "Johnny tell you about the Golden girl and what he thinks?"

"Yes. He thought I should be warned."

"Well," Kelsey confessed, "I think you're right. But if I left this trail I'd be lost in five minutes."

"I can get us through."

"Then take the wheel and pick your own heading."

Teal nodded. There was sureness in the way she read the country and pressed through. They came finally to a place where she said, "We can ford the river here." They crossed the stream without trouble at that point, then began a long and twisting climb to a tableland. The muscles of her face lost their tension, and out of a growing sensitivity to her feeling he also began to relax.

Later they came to the edge of the wheeling prairie, passing into a stand of timber. The horses showed the effects of the hard ascent. Teal reined in, saying, "There's not so much hurry now. Let's loosen the cinches and let the horses rest a while. They always remind me of fat women in corsets when it's hot."

He laughed. "That's a kind of being cooped up I don't reckon you'll ever need."

"Thank you, and I hope you're right."

Dismounting, they loosened the saddle latigos, trailed reins, and seated themselves near the horses to rest. Stark yet oddly attractive country ran to the horizons, brown land that swelled and dipped, a piece of great prairie strangely flung down in this mountain

26

country. Plowland, he thought. The plow had always been the enemy of the hunting arrow.

He rolled a cigarette and sat smoking. Teal looked at him from time to time. He had a sense of complete ease with her, for she was unlike any woman he had ever known. He knew already from her little ways and actions that she was a girl of strong feeling, and that much of it was feeling unknown and unsuspected by the common run of her sex.

Aware that he was stirring emotions he had best leave alone, he ground out his cigarette. He said, "Irish, you're a mighty attractive girl. I bet you're going to have trouble finding a man who'll fit your scheme of things."

"What made you say that?"

"Just been thinking my own long thoughts."

"You having trouble finding such a person?"

"Oh, no."

"This girl you're meeting—is she the girl, or just a girl?"

"It's not decided for sure."

"Not in your mind, anyhow," she said.

"My turn. What made you say that?"

"I learned to read signs before I learned to read print."

"Like an Indian?"

"As an Indian."

He gave her a bewildered stare. "What do you mean?"

"I'm only half Irish," she said. "And half Nez Percé. I thought if I dropped enough hints you'd guess."

CHAPTER THREE

THEY rode on, Teal directing their course through a series of draws and canyons that she seemed to know so well that she was never in doubt. Kelsey quit trying to keep his bearings, placing in her a complete trust and thinking how odd that was, since the blood in her was by its nature supposed to be hostile to the blood in him. They traveled west steadily now, shaded in the bottoms and with the lowering sun blazing in their faces when they topped out onto a section of yellow knolls.

By the time they reached the place where Teal said they would separate, the sun had set. By then they were in flatter country where forested hills cut a wide arc to the south. She reined in and nodded toward the upthrusts.

"If you keep on that way," she said, "you'll come to Grangeville. Mount Idaho's only three or four miles down the trail from there."

"Teal," he said, "it's none of my business, but I've got to know more about this. Johnny said your father's name was Mick Shannon. Where is he?"

"Dead. I don't even remember him. He was a soldier once, like you. When his enlistment ended, he went to work for Johnny Hite. Johnny liked him so well they were soon partners. And he wasn't a squaw man. He and my mother were married at the Lapwai mission."

"That don't matter to me."

"It does to me."

"Then I'm glad that's how it was. Your mother went back to her people after your father died?"

Teal nodded. "She married again, as an Indian woman has to. I have brothers and sisters. I lived with them till I was twelve. Then Uncle Johnny wanted to send me to school. I was excited about it then. But now I'm kind of sorry."

"This is an awful risky time for you to be visiting with them. Lord knows what's going to happen."

"My family belongs to the village of Looking Glass. His is the least hostile of the nontreaty bands, but he's roaming with the other chiefs—Joseph, White Bird, and the rest." Teal smiled gravely. "The Indians who ran away from you last night were two of my brothers with some friends. They say Looking Glass has decided not to take any part in a war."

"Why'd they run away from me?"

"Johnny made them go because they don't share Looking Glass's feeling. They're angry and resentful and they want to stick with the other nontreaties. Johnny knew it would be a white man coming and was afraid something might happen." Teal looked north, adding, "My people are only a few miles off in that direction. I'll be all right. Good-by."

"Wait!" he said anxiously. "What if you're caught in the trouble? Teal, have your visit, then get back to Johnny's. Promise me that."

"I can't." Her eyes, searching his face, were warm with something he could not name. "Luck, man, with your horse ranch, and lots of space and air and sky. I'll wonder about that."

"Don't go!"

But she did, starting her horse and cutting out from him and not looking back. He sat watching until the ground swells swallowed her, deeply puzzled and disturbed, and there was a notable emptiness where she vanished. Then he swung his own horse but rode slowly. Something had come and gone, like a light across the sky, and he knew that their lives might never touch again. Perhaps it was better so. A man had to build a solid and practical life for himself. He'd laid too much groundwork to make giddy changes now, and he had a mission to fulfill in Mount Idaho.

Even before he entered the village of Grangeville, he was aware of excitement. There were several frame houses and business places, with one large structure that stood out. This building had been stockaded with logs. Sacks of something buttressed the windows of the upper floor. They expected trouble or had had it here.

The rest of the town seemed empty, but a team and wagon stood before the gate of the stockade. Men in the rough clothing of settlers were congregated about, and they were watching him closely as he rode in.

"For Gods sake!" a man called. "Did you come through from Lewiston?"

"Crossed over from the Clearwater. What's wrong?"

"If you ain't found out, buck, you're lucky." The settler rid himself of tobacco juice and wiped his mouth with the back of his hand.

Kelsey thought first of the Goldens and wondered if word of that had somehow reached this far-off place already. Johnny Hite had been worried about that. The Riskin brothers, who had caught and shot the supposedly guilty Indians, would want to brag about their exploit, Johnny had said; both were the breed of cat that always did.

"Well, what happened?" he said.

"Wagonload of settlers jumped last night and butchered. Between here and Cottonwood."

"Sure it was Indians?"

The settler stared at him. "Well, *that's* a crazy question. Was it Injuns? Who else you think it would be?"

"I don't know anything about it, man."

Jerking a thumb over his shoulder, the settler said, "Go in the Grange hall and ask your silly question. Some lived. One's a woman, shot through her hips. Ask her who done it. Who are you, anyhow, buck?"

"I come from Montana, friend," Kelsey said mildly.

"Well, Lew Day, he tried to get through to Lewiston. Redskins shot and wounded him, but he got back to Cottonwood. The nontreaties have got their camp close to there. The folks in Cottonwood figured it was time to get out. Loaded up in Ben Norton's wagon and started out. Caught about halfway. One woman was taken prisoner. We didn't know about it till this morning, when Frank Fenn stumbled onto a kid that got away and hid."

"I'm persuaded," Kelsey said, feeling cold and ill as the impact registered. Johnny and Teal had got him confused, but this was a deadly thing of open and frightening portent. The Cottonwood Indian camp had been Teal's destination. This thing had come out of her people and been inflicted on his own and was something she could not deny and defend. "What next?" he asked the tight-faced group about him.

"Well," said the talkative settler, "we're waiting for the Army to get here, where it should of been a week ago. We're organizing a platoon of volunteers. Care to sign up?"

"Sorry, but I got business that won't keep in Mount Idaho."

"Same thing there. Settlers are all coming in off the prairie as fast as they can travel."

Kelsey's cheeks were stiff as boards as he rode on. Concern for Glenna now filled him, and he wondered how much trouble they would have before they were safely out of here and on their way home. It might prove difficult to get out at all if the Army kept on bumbling around.

The shadows of evening flowed down from the mountains as he rode into the second and larger town. He was not surprised to see the tangle of wagons that filled the open spaces and the number of horses picketed on vacant lots and around the edges of the town. On a hill north of the settlement a large force of men was at work on another stockade.

It was not hard to pick out the hotel. Arrived before its stubby porch, he saw from the congestion within that his chances of getting a room for himself were not good. He swung down, trailed the reins of his horse, and started into the place. At the door he came against a man who was trying to crowd his way out. They stared at each other in dawning recognition.

"Kelsey Ames!" the man said loudly. "Howdy, man! And you're just the kind of huckleberry we're looking for. But there's no use going into that beehive if you're after a room. I just tried."

"Mainly I'm looking for a girl, Sim."

"Then you've got your pick of Camas Prairie. It looks like they're all here." Sim Temple was a horse trader who lived in Lewiston, and he grinned. "See you?"

"Pretty soon."

Kelsey went on inside. He saw at a glance that everything was completely disrupted. The lobby's chairs were filled, and bedding scattered about attested that even floor space was scarce at night. There was a short, high desk, but nobody was in attendance. He swung the register around and searched back several days without finding Glenna's entry. With the feeling that something was squeezing his lungs, he turned about and left the place to find Sim Temple waiting in front. Tightly he said, "You heard anything from Slate Creek, Sim?"

"That where your lady was coming from? Well, there was news come in today. They caught their first trouble day before yesterday, in that lonesome country on the Salmon above Slate Creek. The redskins rode from one ranch to another. Report is they killed half a dozen men. The rest are forted up in town, same as they're fixing to fort up here."

"I've got to get down there, man."

"Now, you wait. You're lucky you got this far alive, and even the Clearwater trail ain't safe. It'd be suicide to try and go down the Salmon. The Injuns got hold of whisky when they looted a saloon somewhere down there. They've tasted blood, and we've got to smash 'em before it goes any further."

"What's the Army in the country for?"

"Go ask General Howard. He laid down the law. He made the tough talk. And he's still setting there at the fort with four-five hundred troops. So we've got to do it ourselves, and we're organizing a company of volunteers. Sign up, man, and we'll get it done. I know how you feel. I got my own family in Lewiston. But I ain't trying to get home till I'm sure they're going to be safe."

"What do you figure on doing?" Kelsey said. "Jump their camp at Cottonwood?"

"I ain't trying to run it," Temple said, "and I don't know what they plan. Ad Chapman was elected captain. He's a squaw man who lives on the White Bird. His woman's a Umatilla, and he ain't got any love for the Nez Percés, but he knows 'em. He had old Looking Glass in town here today."

"Looking Glass?" Kelsey asked, remembering that was the chief of Teal's own village. "Had him here?"

"The old coot's pulled out and he's going home to the Clearwater. But he says war can't be avoided now. The other chiefs were kind of on the fence about it, themselves. Then some young hotbloods went out and made certain their chiefs didn't give in to Howard. They done the work on the Salmon, then caught the Cottonwood wagon. They want the Army to try and do something about it."

In spite of his worry and seething anger, Kelsey was relieved to know that Teal would have to go back to the Clearwater to find her people and would not be at the Cottonwood encampment when it was attacked. No settler worth the name had ever lived who would wait for his family to be butchered when he could go on the offensive himself.

Another thing contradicting his sudden fury against the Nez Percés was a question that still lay naggingly deep in his mind. He said, "Sim, you ever hear of the Riskin boys?"

"Chappy and Billy? I sure have."

"Who are they?"

"God knows. Ask me what, and I'll tell you. They're a pair of renegades and a pair of squaw nailers."

"What's that?"

"They like squaws, and they like it better when it comes reluctant."

"Ah," Kelsey said, on a long, slow breath. "They ever known to go after a white woman?"

"Not that I've heard of. But they would if they figured they could get away with it like they can with the squaws. Why?"

Kelsey told him what he had found on the Hell Gate trail, what the Army corporal had told him and Johnny Hite, and what Johnny thought about the Riskins.

"And likely Johnny's right," Temple said promptly. "Them bastards seen the chance to do it and lay it onto the Injuns. By God, they ought to be hanged. But how can a man prove what he thinks?"

"That's a lot of trouble, Sim, just to take a woman.

Johnny figured there was more than that, I think. And I'm beginning to wonder. The treaty Indians on the reservation haven't shown any signs of helping the nontreaties, have they? But they're apt to get hot under the collar about them two bucks—shot and accused of that crime by white scum like the Riskins."

"They're mighty apt to. But what white man would want to egg them into it? The Riskins are trouble-makers, but why would they go that far? It makes more sense that they seen this pretty girl in camp and done it on the spur of the moment."

"I hope you're right," Kelsey said.

CHAPTER FOUR

KELSEY picketed his horses on the grass outside of town and managed to get his evening meal at the hotel. The ring of axes and the thump of mauls came through the night as work was pressed on the stockade. Within the hotel women were at work molding bullets. The deepening darkness was a deepening of tension that nobody could quite conceal. Kelsey had learned by then that Loyal Brown, founder of Mount Idaho and now leading its defenders, had sent an urgent request for troops to Fort Lapwai.

General Howard had moved up from departmental headquarters at Vancouver. He must have expected resistance to his flat ultimatums, for he was heavily supported, with Companies F and H of the First Cavalry, G of the Twenty-first Infantry, and two other cavalry troops he had established in a cantonment west of the Snake. Chapman's company of volunteers had decided to wait for word of Howard's immediate intentions before it took action.

The feeling was general that one prompt show of such a force would quickly end the growing Indian uprising. Much as he wanted to share it, Kelsey remained skeptical and tight with apprehension. He slept that night with his horses, torn between his desire to break through to Glenna at any risk and his feeling that he had ought to lend his help to settle matters permanently.

The next morning he learned that a few more settlers had reached the town during the night. There were now around a hundred refugees in Mount Idaho. The stockade was taking shape, a large circular structure of two parallel fences with logs and rock piled between. A gap on one side had been filled with sacked flour, for lack of other materials.

Then Kelsey's choice between independent and concerted action was made for him. Word came that the Nez Percé had broken up their lake encampment and were moving in force into White Bird Canyon. Although that was somewhat reassuring to the town, it raised an instant alarm in Kelsey. The White Bird lay between Mount Idaho and Slate Creek, so that the lessened danger to one only increased it for the other.

Finding Temple, he said, "I'm joining your outfit, Sim. We've got to get a move on."

Temple nodded. "But not go off half-cocked. Brown's half-breed messenger got back from Fort Lapwai. Two cavalry companies pulled out last night.

Chapman's taking us boys to Grangeville to meet 'em. Likely we'll go right on from there after the Injuns."

The regulars out of Fort Lapwai reached Grangeville at sunset, two understrength troops. Waiting boredly with Chapman's volunteers, Kelsey saw at first glance that they were mostly raw recruits. The long march had already worn them down, and punished their horses even worse.

Chapman went into conference with the Army officers at once. Captain Perry commanded the regulars, and he had with him a young lieutenant wearing Infantry insignia. Puzzled by that lone foot-slogger, Kelsey asked a trooper about it.

The private grinned. "That's Theller, and he volunteered for this stinking job. Beats me why he did. He left the prettiest young wife you ever seen at the fort."

Word was soon passed that Perry meant to press on at once in pursuit of the traveling Nez Percé. The column moved out, the volunteers leading, with the regulars strung out tiredly into the rearward dusk. Temple rode beside Kelsey. Grinning, the man said, "I want you real close, Ames. I don't know the first thing about soldiering and I'm getting scareder every minute."

"Then what do you know about the White Bird?"

"Man, it's rough. Takes hours just to get down into the canyon from the hill. I got a snake in my belly that keeps telling me it might be even harder to get out."

At the walking gait enforced by the worn cavalry horses, it took two hours to bring the command to the summit of the great hill it had to cross and descend.

Chapman fell back for another consultation with Perry, then the order was passed along the line to halt for a rest period. The command was by then in white pine, under a blazing blanket of stars. Cinches were to be loosened, the horses picketed under close guard. Except for the sentries, the troops could sleep, but nobody was to smoke or strike a match.

Stretched out in what was reminiscent of many another bivouac, Kelsey heard the old familiar sounds of hushed men's breathing, of horses stamping or breaking off mouthfuls of grass. He was too keyed up to achieve more than an alert somnolence and was instantly aware of it when, somewhere in that halt, some fool trooper or volunteer struck a match.

Kelsey's curse of warning was echoed all about. The light went out, but from the distance came a raven's *"Quoah . . . quoah. . . ."* The timing had the effect of a rifle shot on Kelsey's nerves. He knew that somewhere close ahead keen ears had heard the signal and relayed it farther on. He trusted Ad Chapman to realize they were under close surveillance and might run into a trap.

The command was aroused a little before dawn, not by a bugle call, but by the toes of rough boots. Grumpy men gnawed hardtack and drank thirstily from their canteens, fatigue and tension having parched them. Walking out from the camp to relieve his restlessness, Kelsey took a look about. Northward the green mountains and brown hills rolled down. Blue-misted canyons creased the lower land wherever the country broke open enough to give a view. The forward country was cut from sight by timber.

Jaded and truculent, the command assumed its set pattern of march and lined out on the trail. It worried Kelsey that, instead of keeping scouts well ahead of the main body, Perry seemed satisfied to have Chapman and his volunteers spearhead the march only a few hundred yards in advance.

At last Kelsey said to Temple, "If I had charge of this outfit, I'd figure out the most unlikely thing that could happen and get set for that and nothing else."

"Think they'll 'bush up?"

"They'll do what we're not looking for, and we're barreling down this hill like we were going to the fair."

Temple scratched the lean line of his jaw. "I heard a sergeant and lieutenant talking. They figure Chief Joseph's rushing for that wild country below the Salmon. Perry wants to catch him before he makes it. This is rough, but the country down there is worse."

"Joseph knows that better than Perry does."

"So what?"

"So he's apt to make his fight, if he wants one, in country he'd seem likely to pass up."

The going, that morning, proved even worse than Temple had warned. The command had only the worn and ancient Indian trail to follow. The route ran down elbow after elbow, occasionally offering glimpses of deep canyons and timbered hogbacks. That went on for three or four hours, Kelsey estimated; then suddenly the trail bottomed out, the mountain giving way to Idaho's eternal green-brown hills.

Even he was reassured by the country that immediately confronted them, for the trail struck out along a long, flat, and rocky ridge. Except for a cluster of rocky buttes ahead and below, there was nothing but air and sky about.

"We'll soon be down on the crick," Temple said, "and out of this."

Ad Chapman was out front, the Army bugler riding near him. Suddenly Chapman raised his weight onto the stirrup leathers and then spurred forward. He spoke no order, but the bugler followed, then the rest of Chapman's particular detachment. For a reason Kelsey could not yet divine, the volunteer captain was making a bold, direct charge toward the nearing buttes across the forward trail.

Whatever he had seen and however foolish his sudden, silent rush, it drew from the looming buttes a chilling eruption of sound. Hidden men loosed a storm of bullets and a hail of arrows. Still the stubborn Chapman drove his horse straight forward. But the bugler threw up his arms and fell dead from the saddle. Bewildered and uninstructed, the volunteers and regulars riding with them tried to follow Chapman.

"That's no rear guard!" Temple yelled at Kelsey. "It's the whole damned shebang! What's Ad up to, goddamn him? Trying to get us butchered?"

It was a case, Kelsey thought bitterly, of somebody playing soldier without quite knowing what he was doing. After that first widespread, determined volley, there was a brief quiet. As if finally regaining his reason, Chapman whipped his horse about. His detachment followed in a full thundering retreat along the ridge.

The main command milled in disorder, men cursing, yelling for orders, and cursing again. Those who could mount rose to saddle, only to be baffled as to what to do. The ones with loosened cinches struggled desperately to get back aboard. Even trained, disciplined minds, Kelsey knew, were subject to shock. Soon an order rang out.

"Spread across! Anchor on the draws and form a line! Horse holders fall back!"

The volunteers took position on a lower knoll that commanded the vicinity immediately about them. From his position, Kelsey could see that the regulars had been whipped into the semblance of a skirmish line, its flanks resting on the tops of two parallel ravines that rose toward them. It was a weak position, but the best at hand. The over-all situation was too grimly similar to one he had been in on the flats across the Little Big Horn, for the only retreat was up the twisting, pitching trail they had descended with such effort.

Then the distant thump of massed hoofs rang out. The hostiles were not pulling out, content with one withering assault. Kelsey saw a party of mounted warriors, stripped for action, whip into the draw on the command's left flank. It was visible only until the bulge of the land cut it from sight. It was thundering up the draw, protected and trying to outflank the enemy and cut off the one chance of escape. Then the Indians came into view as they topped out of the draw. They bent on the blind side of their ponies, firing as they streaked past.

The command opened up as one man. But on the level ground they had reached, the hostiles could wheel out of range. They melted into the scattered rocks, seizing positions where they could harry escape up the trail.

Before the impact of that grave turn had fully registered in Kelsey, a second and larger war party came boiling up the low saddle ground on the command's other flank. Again the command could only watch in impotent fury and dread. This bunch also hung on the far side of its horses while it topped out to loosen wicked fire. Kelsey saw a cavalry mount sink slowly, then fall over. He heard the startled, protesting outcries that meant hits among the troops. The second party of warriors also blended into the rocks. Within minutes, the command was subjected to a deadly mass fire from all sides.

"If I weren't on the wrong side," Temple called, "I'd admire that."

Kelsey himself felt a grudging respect for the skillful planning and the discipline with which the ambush had been brought off. This place that had seemed so unlikely had been perfect for it. A withering, unrelenting fire now poured into the troops, who met it with a hot and stubborn fire. But the situation was hopeless, and every man there knew it well.

Somewhere a man yelled, "I'd rather be a live coward than a dead hero! Why don't we get out of here?"

The voice was a volunteer's, and it was as if it had carried an official order. Men rose all about and made for their horses and tried to go up to leather. Many of them fell, and over on the regulars' line the same thing started, turning the situation into a sudden rout. Taunts and cries of triumph came from the Nez Percés. Men who had managed to seat themselves in saddles drove for the climbing trail.

There was nothing to do but follow suit, and Kelsey swung to his horse and went up. Clearing their own position, the volunteers overran the regulars, charging through the mill. The leading horses were streaking for the point where the trail, more defensible, climbed off the ridge. The weight of numbers carried most of them through, giving hope to those that followed. Dust and powder smoke fouled the air, while the crackling of guns and the wicked swish of arrows were everywhere. The Nez Percés burst out of cover to close in.

After that it was a milling, mixed-up rout. Each man fought for himself and his own escape, while the Indians also fought independently, adding knives now to their bows and guns. In the chaos, Kelsey could do nothing but seek his own escape, cutting and veering, shooting and riding for the trail that rose up the mountain.

About a mile from the deserted battleground, five cut-off troopers left their saddles and fled into the rocks. They were instantly lost in the swirling melee of figures and dust. Others were unhorsed, their mounts caving under them, and these were left to fend for themselves. Except to shoot his way through, no man had time to fight. The Indians still mixed in, while others drove tirelessly at the flanks and rear. They had a wheeling tactic, cutting close to fire, then whipping away to reload, so that the wear on the fringes was constant.

A second group, their horses played out, finally dismounted to fight. The mill swallowed them. When the retreating command reached the narrows at the start of the trail, Lieutenant Theller fell back with a detachment to put up a gallant rear-guard action. The fate of his entire detail was soon evident. The Nez Percés kept coming on.

At last the pounding, beaten command was on the twisting trail that took so long to climb to the summit. By then a third of it was gone and half the remainder weaponless. No chance now to make a stand, to save the day. Pressed every foot of the way, the command never halted, never did more than fire back across its shoulders. And thus it was chased back across the summit of White Bird hill and half the way to Grangeville. It was the Nez Percés that broke it off, satisfied with their efforts.

Though scattered now from the rest, Kelsey and Temple had managed to stick together. When at last they could rein down their heaving horses, they dismounted and looked at each other and felt no need for comment.

At last Kelsey said, "Don't take it too hard, Sim. I went through exactly the same thing once before with Major Reno. We were sent into a situation that hadn't been appraised. We got the hell shot out of us and we ran like monkeys with turpentine on our tails."

"Hell, I can take a beating," Temple said. "It ain't

that. You know as well as I do what this means. They're blooded, and they've pulled off a whale of a victory. If they ever had any hesitation about a full-scale war, it's gone now. It'll kindle a fire in the treaty Injuns and on every other reservation in the country."

"I know, Sim. What are you going to do now?"

"Try and get home to Lewiston and look after my own family. I wasn't much worried about them until now."

"And I've got to get to Slate Creek."

Temple stared. "You want to go back through that canyon?"

"No other way to get there?"

"Not unless you go the long way round by Florence and cut over the hump."

"Then I'll go the long way round."

"Luck, then," said Temple, offering his hand. "I'm on my way from here. I couldn't stand to see the folks in Mount Idaho when their boys come marching home."

They shook hands, and then Temple was gone, riding out upon the lonely plain.

CHAPTER FIVE

STANDING in lonely detachment among the evergreens of the mountains, Florence was still a relaxed town, informed of the trouble across the ridges, concerned and ready to help, but so far safe from the growing Indian rebellion. A boom placer camp in the previous decade, the richest in central

Idaho, it had lost pace but not its lusty vigor. Kelsey Ames rode onto the main street from the Mount Idaho trail too restless to put up for the night, yet uneasy about striking on into the deeper mountains in the approaching darkness.

He was passing the hotel when a girl on the broad and shadowed porch looked up in sudden interest and then let out a cry.

"Kelsey! Kelsey!"

He stared and gasped, "Glenna! What on earth are you doing here?"

Hurrying toward him, a slender girl in whipping skirts, she abruptly reflected his surprise. "You didn't get the letter I sent you at the Mount Idaho Hotel?"

He shook his head, dazed by the unexpectedness of it and his surging relief. He swung from the saddle as she ran up, and they grasped each other in hungry fierceness, unabashed by the onlookers. When she stepped back, his eyes devoured her.

She fed them well, a lithe and animated girl whose eyes and hair were brown, whose mouth was warm and smiling.

"Then it's a good thing," she said, "that I've spent the last two days sitting on that porch watching the Mount Idaho trail for you. I was worried to death."

"You had nothing on me, honey." He nodded toward the hotel. "You got a room there? I'll be up as soon as I've taken care of these cayuses."

"I won't let you out of my sight again. Come on."

She walked with him, holding onto his arm, as he led his horses down the dusty street toward a livery barn he had spotted. Questions and answers boiled out of them both. She had got out of Slate Creek just ahead of the trouble. Her uncle, who had married Trace's sister, had grown increasingly alarmed over the actions and attitudes of the Salmon Indians, and had suggested a change of plans after she had written her father to have Kelsey pick her up at Mount Idaho. Instead, she had been brought to Florence, which was a far safer place to wait.

"Your letter was probably at the hotel in Mount Idaho," Kelsey told her. "I never asked. Couldn't even get a room there, and everything was topsy-turvy. There's over a hundred settlers forted up there."

"The best part is," Glenna said, "we can go home over the old south trail to Bannock and not have to go near the trouble again."

He shook his head regretfully. "I've got to go to Lewiston."

Alarm instantly leaped into her features. "But why?"

"Business. I've got to see Lafe Halverson for your dad and pick up a batch of new horses. We can go by way of the Clearwater, but I don't think the prairie's too dangerous right now. The Nez Percés are moving down into the Salmon."

"Couldn't the business keep? I'm so anxious to get home!"

"I don't think we ought to high-tail it just because there's a war."

"Maybe you're ashamed to run, but I'm not, mister! The last couple of weeks have been terrible!"

"You can bet I won't run any risks with you."

He put up the horses, aware that he had disappointed her in her desire to flee home to Montana. But he did not mean to drop a good half of his business over here simply because the situation had grown more dangerous than expected. Moreover, he was not eager to get her home too soon. They needed time together, away from old haunts and old influences.

He was privately pleased when the room he drew at the hotel was right next to Glenna's. He scrubbed up, got into the change of clothes he had brought along, and began to respond to this town's relaxed and casual atmosphere. Then he rapped on Glenna's door, and they descended to the dining room together and had supper. At the end of the meal, the trouble seemed far away from them.

"You haven't really told me hello yet," he said afterward. "Let's go up to your place."

"Let's."

Then, as he closed her door behind them, she ran into his arms to give back more nearly what he wanted, the hunger engendered by weeks of separation and whetted by mutual worry. "Missed you, missed you!" she whispered huskily. "And how's Dad?"

"Told me to get the lead out and marry you."

"Why don't you?"

"Here? Will you come and find a preacher with me right now?"

She laughed merrily. "Not that soon, darling. But we've got to quit being foolish. We can get together. I know we can."

"If I'd just give in?"

"Kelsey, we're not going to start quarreling already. I've come to see some things differently since I've been away."

"Then you ought to stay away from Butte another year or two."

"That's why you're in no hurry to get home?"

"One reason, if you want the truth. I haven't come to see a thing differently while you were gone. I love you, and want to marry you, but I won't do it at the cost of turning my life over to Trace Buckmaster to run the way he runs yours. Even if it does mean stepping into his shoes someday and being a rich man. I just wouldn't like the life."

"I understand that, and I still think we can work it out." She stood before him, her head lifted. A smile built itself on her mouth and impulsive arms came up to close again about his neck while her warm and pliant body pressed hard against his own.

"That's practically criminal assault," he said against her mouth. "We'd better go and get the knot tied."

"Soon as we're home."

"Then the hell with formalities."

He heard the musical notes of her laugh and in an explosion of wild delight caught her up and carried her to her bed. Her eyes were closed as he put her down, and she accepted him in the space beside her. The scent of her hair and the warmth of her wrapped themselves about him. But as he reached for her, she raised her hands between them and gently pushed him back.

She whispered, "Easy, man—and patience."

"No!"

"Just hold me. Tell me it's going to be all right between us."

"If we start off right, it will. Let's start."

"Mind me, or I'll make you leave." Her head came onto his arm, and she emitted a sigh of contentment. He knew that negation had risen in her with finality, although desire still stained her cheeks and showed in her eyes and the unsteadiness of her breath. Yet she accepted this much of new intimacy, which was gain and proof that his best chance of capturing her undivided devotion lay in keeping her as long as possible to himself.

"I'll mind as far as Lewiston," he told her. "But no farther. And we'll light out for there bright and early in the morning."

"All right."

It was an odd thing, he thought as they lay quietly in the growing night. When he was with her his interest was riveted absolutely, with no question within himself as to his wants. Only when they were apart or together with her father did he grow restless and inclined to questions that had no answers. He began to wonder if this were not because she had actually given him very little of her private and innermost self. Maybe she understood that and was doing this to show him why she felt they could work out their lives with success.

ALSO a product of the placer stampede, Lewiston now lay in comparative lethargy where the Clearwater met the Snake. Gone were the muslin shanties and many of the old log cabins. At this June season, with the two rivers in flood, steamboats could come up from the Columbia to lie against the landing floats.

Arrived there with Glenna after a long but untroubled ride, Kelsey let her dismount at the Luna Hotel, then took the horses on to the livery. The hostler did not know if Tooney Bishop had reached Jawbone Flat with the new horses Trace had ordered from him, but he had other news of interest to Kelsey.

Companies of volunteers had been raised in all the towns on the prairie, with more having come in from Walla Walla and Dayton in Washington Territory. To the remnants of the force beaten at White Bird, General Howard had added other troops drawn from Forts Walla Walla, Vancouver, and Stevens. He had taken personal command and was finally in the field with this tremendous force, which enjoyed the extra benefits of Gatling guns, which the Indians feared greatly, and of mountain howitzers.

Kelsey felt some hope that the trouble could be stopped this time, and his spirit was lighter as he walked out to the street. He had Trace's vague, mysterious message to deliver to Lafe Halverson, and he decided to get that off his mind.

The man ran a supply house here at Lewiston, a business he had started when six-guns still ruled the land. Once, Kelsey knew, he and Trace had worked together in a loose partnership, supplying the gold camps in central Idaho and over on the Montana side of the mountains. Halverson was connected with the seaports by way of the river boats and by freight wagons from Wallula and Walla Walla. Trace had handled the harder interior distribution.

When he came to the building, the door to the office stood open for air. He heard a man saying, "No, Ben, no. You leave that end up to Chappy Riskin." As he turned through the door, two men swung to give him an irritated stare. That reaction, more than what he had heard, made Kelsey wonder what he had interrupted.

One man was a stranger to Kelsey, but Lafe Halverson said heartily, "Why, it's Kelsey Ames. It's all right, Ben. This here's Trace's man. You go on now and do what I told you."

Ben went out while Halverson offered his hand. Kelsey accepted it, although he did not like the man and never had. He was heavy, bald, and inclined to sweat in any kind of weather, while his florid, benign face masked one of shrewdest minds in the country. He had made himself rich the same way Trace had, by seizing opportunities wherever they lay and wringing the utmost from them.

"Riskin's a name I don't cotton to," Kelsey said. "He work for you?"

"Sometimes. He's not worth a hoot in hell, except with a pack outfit. And sometimes I need a packer."

"Handy with a gun, too, I hear."

"So, you heard about the two bucks him and Billy beefed."

"More than that," Kelsey said. "I was the first one to come on the girl that yellow scalp belonged to. There's a big question in my mind whether them Indians died fighting or without even knowing what hit them."

Halverson's pudgy lids narrowed. "Meaning?"

"I'm not sure it wasn't Riskin who scalped the girl, then planted it on the Indians after he'd killed them."

Halverson said slowly, "Well. Why do you suppose he'd do that?"

"You'd have to ask Chappy. But I imagine it made the reservation Indians a trifle resentful and restless. If I know anything about them, some of the younger ones have already slipped off to join Joseph. Especially after that beating the Army took. But never mind. I got a message that might make more sense to you than it does to me. Trace said to tell you he's ready to do business at the old stand."

"Knew he would be."

"What's it going to be this time? Supply contracts for the Army?"

"They're breeding a war."

"Which I think somebody's trying to goose a little. You got any further word for Trace?"

"Tell him I'll keep in touch." Halverson's gaze raked Kelsey's face. "And a word for you. I wouldn't spread talk like you just made. Riskin's a tough customer."

"I gathered that, too."

Kelsey walked out without farewell, annoyed and disturbed. He turned down the street and was halfway to the Luna Hotel when he heard somebody yell at him. Looking about, he saw Sim Temple standing across the way.

Cutting across, Kelsey said, "So you made it."

"Connect with your girl?"

"Stumbled onto her in Florence, and she's at the

Luna. Sim, do you know if Bishop's on the flat with some horses for me?"

Temple shook his head. "I was by there today, too."

"He probably joined the volunteers."

"Don't think so. I heard his brother got into a scrape in Walla Walla, and probably Tooney had to go over there. Serves you right. Why didn't you talk Buckmaster into buying his horses from me?"

"Nobody talks him into anything—or his girl, either."

"Squabbling already?"

"More accurate," Kelsey said wryly, "to say we're *still* squabbling."

"So're me and my woman, but we got married, anyhow. More comfortable."

Kelsey laughed, then grew grave again. "Sim, seeing you reminds me of a little talk we had in Mount Idaho about the Riskin boys."

"What about 'em?"

"I told you I thought Chappy might be interested in fomenting trouble on the Indian reservation. You asked me what for, and I didn't have the answer. Wondering if I don't have it now. Maybe somebody else wants it, and Chappy's only picking up a fast buck and a lot of fun."

Temple's eyes held a cool, almost defensive uncertainty. "I'd go and kill the bastard if I knew who it was."

"I'm not able to tell you who—but maybe I can tell you why."

"All right, why?"

"Supply contracts for the Army. It's having to mobilize more and more. If Riskin's connected with anything else like what happened the other day, remember what I told you."

Glenna had already signed for a room at the Luna. This time he was less fortunate and drew one well down the narrow hallway from hers. But when he had washed up, he returned and rapped on her door and was admitted quickly.

"Find out about the horses?" she asked.

"Bishop hasn't got here yet. I'll have to ride out to his ranch tomorrow. It's in the Blue foothills. But I seen a man who thinks Bishop may be in Walla Walla."

"In which case we'll go on home, won't we?"

He shook his head. "The company needs those horses, Glenna. If we went home without them, I'd only have to turn right around and come back."

She shrugged but was obviously disappointed. "Then we'll stay. But I don't think you're unhappy about it."

"To tell the truth, I'm not. How about us getting married here—tonight?"

He saw her back stiffen and he watched color seep into her cheeks. "If you want to get that over just so we can sleep together, Kelsey, I'm not pleased. I want a nice wedding and—well, Dad's planned on that, too. It's his place to put it on, you know, and he'll want to make it quite an affair."

"Dear God, must he come into every plan I try to make?"

56

"He happens to be my father."

"I've never had a chance to forget that, as much as I'd like to. You've always had things fancy, Glenna. But you've got to get used to having 'em otherwise. We can have a good home, but it will be plain and simple."

"And at the hind end of nowhere."

"If I start a ranch," Kelsey said, "I'll have to go where there's still open land for at least part of my range. Trace Buckmaster hates that idea even worse than you do. If I've got to have a ranch, why, he'll set me up on a dandy all ready to roll."

"And what's so wrong about that? I'd call it generosity."

"I'll say. He'll give me anything on earth except his daughter."

"Kelsey, I think you'd better go. We've been under a strain and we're both tired."

He nodded and went out.

THEY were to wait several days before Bishop showed up with the new horses. The delay and enforced idleness wore on Kelsey, and he knew it was even harder on Glenna now that the joy of their reunion had been dulled by the quarrel. They had their meals together and took daily rides up the valley. Otherwise, they kept apart, Glenna in her hotel room and he out about the town.

He suspected that in part she wanted to evade his further insistence on a quick, informal marriage. Aware of that and afraid that any more pressing would bring on real trouble, he did not mention it again. He was beginning to wonder if the things he disliked in her mind were not an intrinsic part of her nature, as much as a reflection of Trace. If that was the case, then they were never going to bridge the gulf between them.

News reached Lewiston that Howard's big expedition was still in pursuit of the Nez Percés in the wild Salmon Mountains, that the Indians were only fleeing and showing no disposition for another fight. That same evening Tooney Bishop arrived with his apologies and word that the horses were ready and waiting to be inspected on Jawbone Flat. He had been called to Walla Walla, as Temple had conjectured.

The next morning Kelsey rode out to the flat, which lay across the Snake from Lewiston. It was a sandy expanse, hemmed in by steep and treeless bluffs. Bishop had made his camp against the river and had the cut of twenty heavy work horses on a picket line. By noon Kelsey had inspected and accepted the lot. He turned over the check that Trace had sent along with him. Bishop agreed to stay with the animals overnight, and Kelsey rode back to town.

When he put up his saddle horse, he received more military news from the hostler. Howard had heard from friendly Indians that Looking Glass, who had detached his band from the other nontreaties before the White Bird fight, was letting some of his younger warriors slip back to rejoin Joseph. Howard had promptly dispatched two cavalry companies for the Clearwater, fearing for his supply lines. Looking

Glass's village had been jumped by surprise, shot up, and burned.

When he heard that, a sick feeling washed through Kelsey. The Army never recognized noncombatants among the Indians. And Looking Glass, he remembered all too well, was the chief of the village to which Teal Shannon's people belonged. She had been there with them. She had been shot-up with the others.

CHAPTER SIX

LEAVING the livery, Kelsey had moved down the street for some distance when he espied Sim Temple across from him. Their shapes against the wall of an old assay office, Temple and another man were talking heatedly. Kelsey went across.

Temple tipped a bitter nod at the stranger and said, "This is Chappy Riskin. He just come down the Clearwater."

The man was oddly built, wide in the shoulders, short-waisted, and with long legs. He acknowledged the introduction only by staring flatly at Kelsey, who felt a ripple go up his back. The man had the eyes of a spoiled horse, wary and eternally hostile.

"He bring the glad tidings about Looking Glass's village getting shot up?"

Riskin's lips peeled back in a mirthless grin. "That's right. We shot the hell out of 'em, and them siwashes are still running. Caught 'em flat-footed, and it was a mighty neat job."

"Nail any squaws?"

Riskin straightened in surprise, for an instant only staring. Then anger jarred through, painting his cheeks and stretching his mouth. "What's that, buck?" he demanded.

"You heard me. And did you catch any yellow-headed ones?"

"What are you trying to say, man?"

"That you're a low-down son-of-a-bitch, and so's your brother."

Sheer amazement held Riskin through what seemed a minute, but the hostility in his eyes steadily deepened.

"And I second the motion," said Temple.

"Stay out of it, Sim," Kelsey said softly. "If what I think about this man proves true, I'm going to kill him. I wouldn't mind doing it beforehand, just on principle."

Temple's concern was strong on his face but his effort to draw a part of Riskin's fire was useless. The man's fierce attention was riveted to Kelsey. A cedar-gripped Colt rode in his holster, and he seemed wrenched with desire to use it. His shoulders lifted. Then he gave out a roar and shot out a balled fist at Kelsey's jaw.

The blow caught Kelsey only half prepared. He rolled with the punch, danced back, and then came in on his own raging drive. A left hook and right cross knocked the man into the street. A forward lunge, and he hit the renegade with his shoulder, both of them spilling into the dust.

With a furious wrench, Riskin rolled over and got on

top, gagging for breath. Bridging his back, Kelsey managed to twist and throw him off, then scramble to his feet. The renegade shoved to a stand, rocking and staring. His gun had not spilled from his holster. Again he stood in a deep and terrible debate, and again, with a choked outcry, he surged forward.

Kelsey could only clinch and hang on as they wheeled, all but lost in the dust. Thus hung up on each other, they turned once about before Riskin lifted an elbow and slashed it at Kelsey's face. Kelsey countered with a solid, straight-driven punch to the belly. As the renegade bent with a retch of pain, Kelsey caught his head, swiveled, and hurled him forward in a flying mare. The man hit the edge of the sidewalk and let out a torn groan.

Bent and gasping in the dust-fouled air, Kelsey only then realized that a crowd was gathering to watch. Rolling over, Riskin got on all fours. Slowly raising his. head, he made a dazed search for his enemy. Kelsey quartered, coming closer. Riskin sprang from all fours, like a wrestler diving in for a hold. His hands caught the back of Kelsey's head and slowly weighted it downward. A knee came up in a full, hard smash to the face. Riskin peeled off with the kick and then came back, bent and weaving, arms and fingers spread. Raising his guard, Kelsey turned a half circle, then they drove together, each loosening a barrage of fists.

Pain spread out from Kelsey's chest, climbed his shoulders, and settled in his head. Sweat and dust burned and blinded his eyes. For seeming minutes he could neither slow Riskin nor get away from him. He began to recognize the telltale ache of fatigue.

The only trace of weakness in this mustang of a man was his inflexibility. Covering his midriff with his elbows, Kelsey let his mouth sag open. He rolled his eyes, but they were keen enough to see the glint of relish in Riskin. In the same second he twisted and drove a fist up and through the renegade's guard. Riskin's knees sagged even as he was hit again. Holding both arms straight out, Riskin backed up. An unseen hitching rack stopped him. He ducked under, still holding up protesting hands and shaking his head.

Slumped and dragging in the choking air, Kelsey studied him. He dared not cross under or over the rack without risking seconds in which he would be exposed to disaster. He began to move down the bar to its end.

"Either fight or run, Riskin!" Sim Temple yelled. "That ain't no woman you've got there!"

The taunt stung Riskin anew, causing him to turn heavily and move along the bar to meet Kelsey. They came slowly, deliberately together, wary and feinting. Twice the renegade tried to draw Kelsey within reach. Then he boiled forward in his set pattern of hard, straight-driven blows.

That return to habit was what Kelsey had waited for. He struck high and hard, putting his last strength into his arm. The blow jarred his own brain as it reached the underslope of Riskin's jaw with a solid thud. The renegade caught a quick spasm of breath, staggered, and went down. He lay still, all but lost in the billowing dust.

"Remember what I said, Riskin," Kelsey panted. "If

I ever find out that what I think is true, I'll kill you."

Brushing through the crowd, he went on down the long street. Entering the Luna, he went immediately to his room and tried to clean up. He could scrub himself and change his clothes, but the battering of his face was there to linger for a while. Shrugging, he moved down the hallway to tell Glenna that they would hit the trail for home in the morning.

She took one look at him as he came through the doorway and gasped, "You've been fighting! What happened?"

As he returned her study, he understood for the first time how deep and shaking were his suspicions. He was convinced that Riskin was trying to increase the Indian trouble in the service of Lafe Halverson. Her own father, Trace Buckmaster, had sent word to Halverson of his readiness to resume the old partnership. Trace had not divulged the contents of the letter he had received from Halverson. Maybe he knew all about what was going on, both above and beneath the surface. Maybe he had sent a verbal reply not out of laziness, but because he had not cared to commit himself on paper.

While Glenna could not possibly have an intimation of that, Kelsey knew that he dared not voice his suspicions of Riskin unless he came by some kind of evidence that he could take to the proper authorities.

With an easy shrug, he said, "Maybe it was just something I needed to get the kinks out of my nerves. We're starting home in the morning."

She was not satisfied with that explanation, but the

announcement swept the question from her mind. Throwing her arms about his neck, she cried, "Oh, darling, I'm so glad!"

"Take it easy there, unless you want to marry me before we leave."

"I do declare, man, you've got a one-track mind."

"But the track don't go anywhere."

"Have faith, darling. It will."

She was restored to the joyous girl he had met in Florence, but he knew better than to crowd again.

Two hours after daylight they had eaten breakfast, gathered up the horses, and were on the eastbound trail. Strung out on gang ropes, the new draft stock made for slow going. It took them two days to reach Johnny Hite's trading post. The old trader greeted them in his usual affable manner. He showed Glenna his spare bedroom, the one Teal had been using on Kelsey's other visit. The thought of Teal depressed Kelsey, but he made no mention of her.

The trader had Kelsey turn the horses into a fenced pasture near the fort where they could be left alone safely. While Glenna refreshed herself from the day on the trail, the men started supper. Curious as Kelsey was about Teal, the kitchen was too close to the bedroom for him to ask questions. Then Glenna came out to insist on helping with the meal. Johnny appreciated that gesture.

"I used to see your daddy, sometimes," he told her. "Them days Trace was only a packer, and he'd come through here. You look like him except to say you're a heap easier on the eyes."

Glenna smiled. "Thank you. They do say I'm a chip off the old block. That's something Kelsey doesn't like very well."

"You fixing to team up?"

"As soon as we get home."

"Well, it's fine for them that likes it. Me, I never was tame enough for a woman to stand very long."

"And that's something about me," Kelsey said promptly, "that Glenna doesn't like very well."

"Well, you better get it all ironed out beforehand. I'm telling you that."

When they had finished supper and the work that followed, Johnny suggested to Kelsey that they take a look at the new horses, and leaving Glenna to her woman's preoccupations, they walked down to the pasture gate through the gathering dusk. Johnny sized up the new freight horses and pronounced them a good lot.

"Thanks," Kelsey said, "but I reckon we come down here because you know I'm uneasy about Teal. Have you heard from her?"

"If you mean that white man's massacre at Kamiah," Johnny said, "Teal come through it. But she lost a brother. She told me she let you know she's a breed. It was something I figured should be left to her to tell."

"Where are they now?"

"The young bucks are joining Joseph. The women, kids, and old ones are hiding out. They're renegades, now that there's been hostilities. They'll be hunted down and butchered, the same as the warriors." Johnny gave Kelsey a long study, then added, "Like to see her?"

"Could I?" Kelsey gasped.

"I could take you to where they're hiding."

"I'd like to. But it wouldn't be safe to leave Glenna alone."

Johnny pointed. "I'll go back. All you got to do is go through that brush below the pasture. Announce yourself as you come out of it or you might get shot." Wiping his mouth, the old man added awkwardly, "I— I reckon I'd better keep it to myself?"

Kelsey shook his head. "She'll be wondering, Johnny. Better tell her. I've never told her about Teal, but I've never deceived her, either."

Kelsey crossed the fence into the horse pasture and went over that to vanish into the timber. When he looked back, Johnny was returning to the fort. The going was difficult in the combined darkness and timber, and the woods kept on so long that Kelsey began to wonder if he had strayed off course. But presently he realized he was nearing the end of the trees.

He had a tight feeling in his stomach, knowing that alert ears had long since picked him up. But they would be waiting to determine if it was Johnny Hite. Cupping his hands to his mouth, he gave the signal he had heard that night on White Bird hill, a raven's cry. He didn't know for sure what it telegraphed, but it was answered promptly, and he went on. Pressing on, he came into a little cove where two Indian lodges stood. Several alert figures stood solidly in front.

"Teal!" he called then. "It's Kelsey Ames."

"Hello. I wondered if I'd see you."

She came forward from the others, still hard to distinguish in the darkness. She now wore buckskin. Her approach was casual, and he wondered if it wasn't even a little hostile until, coming up, she offered her hand. Suddenly he could think of nothing whatsoever to say to her, but she was not prompt to withdraw the strong brown hand.

"You've been some on my mind," Kelsey said finally. "Especially after I heard what happened at Kamiah. Johnny told me about your brother, and I'm mighty sorry."

"Thank you. Come and meet the rest."

He saw that there were three women, besides herself. They had remained wary and hostile. Teal spoke to him in their tongue, then turned to Kelsey and said, "My mother and sisters."

Kelsey started toward them, saw the inadvisability of that, and made a nod to each. Then the older woman began to talk in low and rushing sounds, to which Teal listened intently. When she had finished, Teal glanced at the ground, then looked up at Kelsey.

"You can't expect them to be cordial."

"I don't. And I wonder what she'd say if she knew I joined the volunteers and went into White Bird Canyon."

"That you got what you had coming. And that's what I say, too."

"Maybe," he agreed. "But what did she say?"

"She asked me to tell you that the trouble is in no way our fault. Until the start of this trouble, no Nez

Percé had ever hurt a white person. But all through the years Nez Percés were robbed, murdered, raped, and hanged. Ever since the first white miners came. Looking Glass's village was happy at Kamiah and it meant to keep out of the war. It had new gardens and good milk cows and beef cattle. There was nothing more it wanted but to stay there in peace. Now the gardens are ruined, the cattle run off, the village robbed and burned. Many men are dead, including her son, and many women and old people and children."

"Tell her I know how she feels."

"And you'd better not stay," Teal said. "I'll walk back through the trees with you."

Kelsey wanted to say something to the three figures who stood so motionless by the lodges, but he could think of nothing. Turning, he followed Teal, who had already slipped away toward the timber. She was swift, and she did not pause until they reached the lower fence of Johnny's pasture.

"Luck," she said. "And I'm glad you're going back to Montana."

"I wish you were, too—or anywhere away from this country. You don't belong in it. You're on neither one side nor the other."

"Oh, but I am on one side," she said, and for the first time feeling crept into her voice.

"You'll stay with your family?"

"To the bitter end. Go now, and take care."

"Teal!"

But she was gone, slipping back into the timber and swallowed from sight. He did not call again, but it was a long while before he climbed the fence and started back for Johnny's fort.

Glenna had gone into her room and apparently was asleep, for no light showed under her door. Johnny was sucking on a pipe in the main room. He only lifted his eyebrows and looked grumpy. Kelsey did not have to be told that Glenna knew where he had been and had not liked it.

"Same bunk for me as last time?" Kelsey asked.

Johnny merely nodded.

CHAPTER SEVEN

JOHNNY went out with Kelsey the next morning to get the horses ready to trail. Once they were away from the fort, he said, "Don't waste any time getting home. I learned something after you hit the hay last night. A runner went through on his way to Fort Missoula. He stopped for a change of horses. Howard wants more troops."

"More?" Kelsey gasped. "Hell, he must have a regiment already. What happened, man?"

"Like I expected. After that cold-blooded attack on Looking Glass's camp, Joseph took his warriors outta Howard's trap on the Salmon like there wasn't any army in the country. He's back on the prairie and in Howard's rear, and the whole prairie's wide open. They've got Cottonwood cut off, and Whipple's there with Perry. He's the one jumped Looking Glass, and I wouldn't mind seeing him get a taste of his own medicine."

69

"Johnny, is there any danger of the treaty Indians throwing in with the nontreaties now?"

"Plenty," Johnny said. "And there's plenty danger of its spreading to your side of the mountains. You can put an Injun on a reservation, but you can never make him contented. And that goes for every reservation between here and the Missouri."

EAST of the trading post, the trail climbed on toward the broad belt of mountain pine. Now, in their third day of travel, the new horses handled much better and could make faster time. Riding beside him, Glenna was quiet through the first hours that morning, but he knew that something troubled her.

At last she said, "So you have fun sometimes when you stop at Johnny's place."

"Fun? How do you mean?"

"I understand you know some squaws."

It was the term she chose that riled him. Giving her a flat stare, he said, "Squaws?"

"Well, this breed you went to see last night. They're all the same, aren't they—except that the mixed bloods can be prettier? Is this one nice-looking?"

"Look, Glenna. This one is as nice a girl as you'll find."

"I asked if she's pretty."

"What difference does that make?"

"Hah."

"Teal Shannon," he snapped, "is only a girl I figure is in a hell of a situation. Her people have defied the Army—which means the government—and now they stand to be destroyed. She don't have to throw in with 'em. She's as white as she is red. But what can she do—turn her back on the woman who bore her? What would you do if Trace was on the dodge and being hunted down?"

After a long moment Glenna said, "I'm jealous, that's all. And afraid. That's the type of woman you need. One so fiercely loyal she'd go anywhere with you and do anything. I haven't got that kind of stuff, Kelsey, and I know it."

She was so humbly honest that his anger turned to concern. "Nonsense. You just had it a lot softer all your life. You got trained to expect a lot more than the average person ever hopes to get. Troubles and hardships most of us take for granted scare you. But I'd bet my right arm that if you'd take the jump, you'd come through with flying colors."

"You really think so?"

"If I didn't I wouldn't be so willing to take it with you."

"I love you, darling. I'm sorry I was so nasty about Teal Shannon. I wish her all kinds of luck."

She had opened herself to him more directly than she ever had before. He remembered now the feelings that had troubled him when he had been alone this way with Teal, his undeniable response to her, and his instinctive knowledge that they had natures very much alike. But he had not felt for her this flaming desire to possess and to hold that he felt for Glenna. Maybe that was only because he had never achieved the same degree of intimacy with her. But all that was falling

71

behind with the miles, and he was suddenly at peace with Glenna.

Around one o'clock they entered the timber with its thick carpet of brown needles and its heady smells. When they came to a roadside spring, they halted to eat and afterward rested for an hour. Smoking a cigarette, Kelsey felt his tensions begin to loosen at last. He let his gaze play upon Glenna, stretched lazily beside him on the grass, and felt a rise of tenderness that did not usually color his feelings. Good had come out of their tangle over Teal. It had jarred Glenna out of her complacency, and in her less self-confidence would be a good thing.

The way Trace had raised her, she had never had to be in doubt about the eventual satisfaction of her desires. She was plain spoiled, if a man was honest, but that did not mean that the good in her could not be brought out. But he had to have her to himself to achieve that, and he dreaded taking her back into the aura of her father's all but total influence.

At the start of twilight two days later, the glaciated lifts of the Anacondas showed before them, and they were coming in on Buckmaster's horse ranch on the Silver Bow. Set on a wooded flat, the headquarters were frame buildings kept carefully painted and repaired. As they rode into the place, the new horses ambling ahead, Kelsey noted the speculative way Glenna looked at the place. She seemed to see it through new eyes, as her first home as a bride since he had agreed to live here until he had saved enough to set up for himself somewhere else.

That was a big gain; before she went away, she had been set on living in town.

He dropped off the horses, turning them over to his two punchers; then he and Glenna rode on for Butte. When at last they entered Butte, it was a cluster of glimmering lights, serene and dwarfed by the rearing hill that gave it its name. Trace Buckmaster's showy place was on the near edge of town, a vast house enclosed by iron fences, with iron deers handsomely posed in the yard. There were lights within to indicate that the master was there.

Quietly Glenna said, "Come on in and we'll tell Dad he can go ahead and put on the goldarndest wedding this town ever saw."

"We'd get into an argument."

"You'll try to get along with him, won't you, now that I'm on your side?"

"If he meets me say thirty per cent of the way."

Trace's heavy voice bawled out, "That you, Glenna? Where in hell have you been? I damned near went crazy."

She swung down and fled up the steps then, and Kelsey scowled at the darkness that swallowed her.

Later he went in for the drink that Trace insisted on having. Her eyes shining with happiness, Glenna left them alone in the boar's nest of a room Trace claimed for his private retreat. Over generous helpings of the town's best Scotch, he grinned at Kelsey.

"Well, I'm glad. She wanted you, and I wanted her to have you."

"But are you willing for me to have her, Trace?"

"Why not?"

Kelsey met his eyes, the merest smile tugging at his mouth. "You haven't shown many signs of it. And you should know at the start that she's willing for me to run the show when it comes to my way of life."

"Well, let's try and get along for her sake."

"If you leave us alone, Trace. And one thing else. Lafe Halverson expects the Indian trouble to turn into a general war. He aims to go after supply contracts, and you're throwing in with him. That right?"

"Close enough. Anything wrong with it?"

"Plenty. Halverson's using the services of a bully boy called Riskin. You know anything about him?"

"Never heard of him. Been years since Lafe and me worked together. What about him?"

"I'm not the only one who thinks he pulled a stinking stunt in Idaho to help spread the Indian unrest. And I think he's got more on tap, from what I heard Halverson tell a man named Ben. I hope you look into the thing before you get tied up in it."

Trace was unperturbed, so plainly so that Kelsey doubted he could be privy to what was going on. Shrugging and making a wry smile, Trace said, "Lafe cuts corners. It's a game with him. He's got more money than he'll ever get rid of, but that don't count. He don't really feel good unless things are booming, and he's making it hand over fist. The gold stampede spoiled him. Touched all of us a little, I guess. You were too young to remember when a man could make a fortune in two weeks, and lose it and make another.

It gets into your blood."

"Something I wouldn't want in mine."

"You're different," Trace said. "Just the same, what you do have in your blood runs you, don't it? I'd call it wildness, and that's something that don't fit Glenna and something I figure you've got to curb."

"Don't you try it, Trace."

"As long as you work for me, you'll take orders."

"I wouldn't want that any other way."

"Fine. Let's have another drink."

The next morning Kelsey started to work the new horses, breaking them to the pull chain and jerk line. Tooney Bishop had already topped them out, and it was only a matter of finishing them off. With the help of Bob Owen and Curly Santana, he was monotonously driving an old freight wagon around the horse pasture, a green animal hooked up with a trained one, when he discerned riders coming in to headquarters from the town road.

The smaller figure of Glenna lifted pleasure in him, but he wondered why Trace was along. He had no expectation of being consulted about the plans for the wedding, and Trace didn't leave town much any more, always sending for the men he wanted to see. Swinging down, he said, "You boys can have it for a while," and headed for the house.

Glenna waved to him gaily from the distance, and they were dismounted and in the shade of the porch when he got there. She looked a little uneasy, so, swinging his attention to her father, Kelsey said, "Anything gone wrong, Trace?"

"Oh, no," Trace said heartily. "Glenna and me got to talking at breakfast and decided to come out. I reckon I'll fix this place up a little."

"What's wrong with it?"

"For one thing, there ought to be running water in the house. I kind of figure on a windmill and cistern. The kitchen's got to be built over before a woman would find it handy. We thought we'd look it over."

"Your house," Kelsey said. "Go ahead."

Trace went on indoors, and the instant he vanished, Glenna ran into Kelsey's arms. She gave a contented sigh as she took his mouth, then whispered, "I'd live in a cave with you, darling. But it's his idea and his money, and there's no harm in humoring him."

"But there is in spoiling you. There's already better here than I'll be able to give you for years to come."

"As if things like that matter to me! All I want is you—anywhere and all the time."

Trace poked around the place. Whatever his sudden ambitions for it, he didn't ask what anybody else thought. Trace never did. Finally he said, "Well, I'll get men out here from town. You ready to go, Glenna?"

"I think I'll stay a while."

Trace grinned. "Well, all right, although I don't know that I'll allow courting on company time. You bring her in, Kelsey."

"Don't need orders for that, Trace."

When her father had ridden out, Glenna said, "I'm afraid you'll have to get used to his wanting to do things for us, whether we like it or not. He's not going to change."

"As long as I stay my own man," Kelsey said.

"My man," she corrected. "Are the boys good and busy?"

"They won't bother us."

"Then you're going to do some courting on company time."

CHAPTER EIGHT

IT was more like old times when, on the following Friday, a stablehand larruped out from town with word for Kelsey that Trace wanted to see him on the double. Saddling a horse, Kelsey returned with the man, going at once to the freightyard, where he found Trace pacing the floor of his dingy little office.

"Where you been?" Trace snapped.

"Hunting buffalo. What's up?"

"Plenty. Word just got here, and it's set this town on end. The whole damn Nez Percé nation's on the Hell Gate trail and headed our way."

"But what for?" Kelsey gasped.

"What for!" Trace snorted. "Because they fought the Army to a standstill again and figure they can write their own ticket!"

"Simmer down, man, and tell me about it."

The biggest fight yet to take place in Idaho, Trace recounted, had occurred on the Clearwater. It had been in full force, a bloody two-day battle that had ended with both sides pulling back. Howard's purpose apparently had been to re-form, but it was a mystery why the Nez Percés had chosen to strike across the Bitter-roots.

"The thing's already hit the newspapers," Trace concluded. "It's raised a hullabaloo from here to the East. The Army's lost the government plenty of face, and Washington wants to quit fooling. There's troops on the way from Frisco and Alaska, and the Second Infantry's on its way from Georgia."

"Godamighty."

"Well, you got another job, and that's why I sent for you. You're going to buy every horse you can get hold of before the price goes up." The shock was leaving Trace now, excitement taking its place, for he was a man who functioned at his best in a crisis. "I'll sign a bunch of blank checks for you. Swing down the Missoula, then come up through the Bitterroot Valley. Wherever you find yourself with forty-fifty head lined up, send me word and I'll get me off to fetch 'em in."

"What do I pay?"

"Least you have to. But whatever it is, pay it. The price will be doubled in a week."

"You trying to corner the market, Trace?"

"I'm trying to help the Army, and they're going to need it." Trace grinned. "The cheaper I get the extra horses, the cheaper we can bid on supply contracts."

"You're going ahead with Halverson."

"Look." Trace leaned forward. "When I heard what had happened, I was scared sick, and I still am. We've got more towns and bigger ones on this side of the mountains. Right now we've got a lot less army. That redskin move looks like they hope to take advantage

78

of that. They could clean out the Bitterroot and Missoula valleys right now, with nothing in their way, but detachments at Fort Benton and Shaw and Missoula."

"And you want to beat 'em to the horses."

Trace hit his desk with his fist. "Have I got to draw you a picture? Overnight the thing's ten times as big as it was. It's going to be a job getting it bottled up again, and the Army's biggest field problem is supply. Ain't that right? All right. That's where we came in. Now, you better go tell Glenna you'll be gone two-three weeks. By the time you get back here, I'll have the blank checks ready and you can light out. You can board at the ranches and towns you come to."

Kelsey nodded, still stunned by the appalling change in the situation. Trace had not overdrawn the danger to western Montana. It was practically defenseless, while the Nez Percés had proved themselves a dangerous foe. He was ready to do anything needed of him. He was more than ready to kill any man who tried to add to the conflagration on this side of the mountains.

By the time he reached Deer Lodge, three days later, he had heard a straighter story of what had happened in Idaho. The Clearwater battle had occurred as first reported, but it was only Joseph's coalition of non-treaty Nez Percés who were on the march over the Bitterroots. Progress was unhurried, General Howard was not yet in pursuit, and the Indians had their families with them. Cavalry out of Fort Missoula hoped to stop them before they had come off the mountain trail. It was to be reinforced from Forts Shaw and Benton, and volunteer militia had been formed in all the towns.

Kelsey could breathe more easily. He had already picked up two lots of horses and sent off reports to Trace. He reached Missoula at the end of ten days fully expecting to find a waiting letter putting an end to the horse buying, now that it was known that the situation was not so grave as it had seemed. There was none, although he learned a surprising and reassuring thing that made Trace's venture seem all the more unnecessary.

Aware that their entry into the valley was to be contested, the Indians had sent emissaries to the commanding office at Fort Missoula asking for a powwow, promising to give no trouble if they were allowed to pass through. The offer had been rejected summarily, a fact that the settlers in the valley had not liked at all.

So a separate council had been held and a treaty arranged directly between the Indians and settlers. The Nez Percés had promptly slipped past the military block at the foot of the trail and, as they had agreed, were moving peacefully northward toward the pass, following their old trail to buffalo country on the eastern prairies. The badly outnumbered soldiers had been judicious enough to leave them alone, with the civil militia supporting the settlers' attitude.

That explained much to Kelsey, for he knew that, driven here and there by the military for so many weeks, the Indians must be hard pressed for food. With peace arranged with the civilians, there seemed no reason why they should not reach hunting ground without the bloodshed that had marred their Idaho experiences. It was relieving and reassuring to him, for he knew that Teal must be among the wayfarers.

Since Trace had not called him off the job, Kelsey decided to work his way on up through Ross Hole, then cross the Sapphires and head for home. But he was told that he would find the pickings slim in the Bitterroot Valley, for the Nez Percés were buying horses and supplies from the settlers and paying for them fairly and honestly. It was an old route for them, and they had many acquaintances.

Two days' scouting in the Bitterroot Valley proved that he wasn't going to find a horse worth buying. By the time he reached Stevensville he had decided to call it quits on his own responsibility. At ranch after ranch the reports he had received were reassuring. Even the Nez Percés believed that the war was over and were as anxious to have it so as were the whites. They were going to the Musselshell to make meat, and then they would try to come to honorable terms with the government.

So, put up at the village tavern, Kelsey was thinking of Glenna and the disrupted plans for their wedding and was quickened by the prospect of seeing her soon again. Yet he also experienced the odd thing that so often occurred to him when he was away from her, a nagging restlessness of spirit. And time after time his thoughts strayed to Teal Shannon, who could not be far away from him that night. He wished he could see her.

By the time he reached the juncture of the trail that sprang into the Sapphires, the next afternoon, he knew he was going to take a slightly longer way home than he had first planned. The Nez Percés were still before him, the sign of their camps and marches unconcealed all along the valley, and they had by then crossed the pass into the Big Hole basin. Dangerous as it might prove to be, he could himself follow over, edge the camp widely if it seemed too risky, and follow an even better trail than the one he had contemplated. And somehow he might get a chance to see or hear something of Teal. By then he had a crowding wish to determine how she fared.

It was by then late in the afternoon, and he knew that if he made contact at all, the only relatively safe time to do it was before nightfall. As long as he acted openly and casually, he felt that he could trust the Indians' promise not to bother such settlers as showed no hostility. They had a surprising record of fidelity to their agreements, considering how often they had themselves been betrayed.

So he rode boldly along the trail, outwardly half asleep in the saddle, although tension began to draw tighter and tighter.

He was lowering upon the Big Hole River when it happened without warning. Out of a silence broken only by the dull footfalls of his horse, five warriors materialized from among the trees, their rifles covering him. His heart made a violent slam against his ribs, but with no change in his outward tired indolence he let his horse come to its own stop.

Nodding, he said, "Howdy," and five impassive faces stared back at him.

Uncertainty seeped into his confidence. He didn't so much as know Teal's name in the Indian tongue, but he hoped that he had another watchword. Quietly the warriors had formed an arc across the trail in front of him, and all five rifles were still leveled. He hoped that at least one of these stonily hostile men would understand a little English.

Pointing to his heart, he said, "Hite. Johnny Hite. My friend."

He had expected that they would at least recognize the name of so old and proved a friend, but it seemed to make no impression. The Indians sat their ponies in their peculiar slouching way and only stared back at him.

"One of you understands me," he said frowning. "Who is it? I want him to take a message to the girl called Teal in my language. Johnny Hite trusted her to me for a day's ride. Again he took me to where she and her mother and sisters were hiding. All I want is for you to take a paper to her. She can tell you whether I come here as a friend."

One of the men spoke in a rattling way, another answered, and neither took his eyes off Kelsey.

The first said, "I know girl."

"Thanks," Kelsey said. "Let me write."

He fished into his pocket for a stubby pencil and a piece of the paper on which he had kept count of the horses he had bought. He wrote: "I'd like to see you. Could you come out here? Kelsey Ames." He handed it to the man who had spoken in English, and this one passed it on to another, who dug his heels into the sides of his horse and rode off into the trees.

Kelsey still was not completely reassured. The warrior could be taking his message to the chiefs, and he might find himself a prisoner in greater difficulties even than he had feared. But in a shorter time than he had dared to hope for, he heard a horse coming toward them and moving fast.

He knew it was Teal, even before she broke out of the obscurity of the deeper timber. She still was in buckskin and rode bareback, but her face stood out to him like a star in the night. Whipping up to the group, she regarded him with an open mouth.

"Oh, you shouldn't have come here! You shouldn't!"

"Hello," he said, and could only smile at her.

She spoke quickly to the men who had held him here. They lowered their rifles reluctantly and retired to a distance, but did not move out of sight.

"I hear it's over," he said. "And I wanted to know what your plans are."

Life in the open had tanned her more deeply, and he saw how rough and worn were her hands. She said, "We don't know that. And you've got yourself in trouble. They're afraid of spies, and they won't let you go again until we've broken camp."

"When will that be?"

"Another day or so. We're making lodgepoles. Everything had to be left behind when we moved out from the Clearwater."

"Where are you going from here?"

Teal frowned. "I can't answer questions like that. How do I know, even, that you're not a spy?"

"You know I'm not."

She nodded and smiled a little. "Since you were foolish enough to come here, I'll have to sponsor you. They won't try to arrest you if I take you into camp and to my lodge."

"I'll get away all right."

Her glance flicked to the waiting and watching warriors. "Kelsey, if you try it they'll kill you. Come and don't hesitate about it."

He had not intended to tie himself up so long, but he had no doubt that she was sincere and shrewd in her feeling. They slipped through the trees, the waiting warriors not immediately following.

At last she said, "Did you come here specially to see me?"

"Yes."

"Why?"

"I don't know."

"If you're sorry for me, you needn't be. The chiefs feel that there's a good chance for peace. The old ones, that is. The young ones just don't trust it. Too much has been promised before, and too much has been swept away."

"You're bitter."

"And how could I help it? If you'd been with me the last six weeks, you'd be, too."

"Irish," he said humbly, "there are already some things I'm bitter about. The main one is the part I took against your people at White Bird. You haven't forgiven me, have you?"

"No."

"Then why don't you let them kill me?"

"Because— Well, because."

Presently they edged the timber to see the flat below them where the river bent. By then the barking of dogs and other noises of the encampment had declared it, and as they came onto the sage-studded plateau it wheeled out before them, probably a hundred lodges set up on the far side of the river. Large horse herds were on three sides of the camp.

"Since you worry," Teal said presently, "I'm going to tell you one thing before we get down there that I should not. Before we left Idaho, I heard a chief say that first we must go to the buffalo country to make meat, for we have little food, little of anything at all. Afterward, if the Army will not leave us alone, we may try to join Sitting Bull across the border. That's a deep confidence, Kelsey Ames."

"I'll remember. But must you go with them?"

"What else? I'm a renegade Injun unless the government grants us amnesty. I haven't much hope that it will."

His presence in Teal's company aroused interest at the edge of the encampment that deepened as she led him through. She said, "I'll have to take you to the chiefs and explain and vouch for you, or they won't leave you alone. It was thought last night that a white man had spied on us from the timber."

"This camp isn't in the safest place, Teal."

"My brothers say the same thing. It's old Looking Glass. He's taken charge, and he hopes so strongly for peace he's persuaded himself that it's come. The young men want to scout the backtrail so they can ambush the Army if it's trying to follow us. We haven't anything but outguards such as you ran into." She looked at him quickly, adding, "I'm telling you things that could be very dangerous to us."

"Why are you?"

"Your concern has pleased me. I feel I can trust you." Teal smiled. "And you're not going to get away from here until we've broken camp."

There was nothing to distinguish the tepee at which she stopped. A flap lifted, a woman peered out, and Teal spoke a few swift words. In a moment a man stepped through the opening in the stretched buffalo hide. He was solidly built, his black hair parted low on the right and hanging before thick shoulders in long, slender braids. He wore a checked shirt and an open vest, and there was a knife in his belt. His face was strong and intelligent, and his eyes brightened as he looked up at Teal while she talked.

When she had finished, she looked at Kelsey to say, "Chief Joseph. Sometimes in command and always our leader. I told him the truth, and he's weighing you against it."

When Joseph answered it was out of the sonorous depths of his chest and very briefly.

"He'll take my word," Teal interpreted. "You won't be bothered if you stay until we leave."

"Tell him I thank him."

"He's curious about your hat and shirt."

"Tell him the truth there, too, and ask if I'd be fool enough to wear them if I'd come to do mischief."

Joseph merely grunted when Teal had spoken,

turned, and disappeared into his tepee. She swung her pony, and Kelsey followed her on along the rows of lodges. Near the upper edge of the camp, Teal stopped at a lodge and motioned to the one next door.

"My mother and sisters are here. My brothers sleep there. You'll share that one with them tonight. Are you hungry?"

Remembering the reception he had got from her family at Johnny's fort, Kelsey was not too comfortable as he swung down with Teal. He also recalled what she had said about the shortage of food.

He said, "Not very. What about these horses?"

"Running Wolf, my next oldest brother, will take care of them."

She bent, ducked through the tepee flap, and held it open for him. He had never before entered an Indian home. There was little to make this place a home beyond mats, robes, and blankets, and a few portage and cooking baskets. There was a small fire in the center of the surprisingly large space, its smoke escaping through the lodge's top. A woman was at the fire, while a girl was stretched out asleep. The woman stared up in astonishment.

Teal spoke to her and was answered. Meanwhile, Kelsey studied the mother, seeing a face that might well have held beauty for Mick Shannon, and a body less rounded with fat than most Indian women's. Teal spoke again, and this time there was relenting in the mother's face.

"She says you're welcome," Teal reported.

"I doubt that."

"She'd flatly refuse to feed you if she didn't mean it. See? She's fixing food."

Teal went out while Kelsey ate something he recognized as a gruel made of corn and some kind of meat, and he had an idea she was out selling him to the rest of her family. The sleeping girl stirred, muttered a little, but did not awaken. The mother's quick look telegraphed instantly to Kelsey that this daughter was ill. Teal returned just then and, noting his puzzled inspection, said, "Her husband was killed on the Clearwater. She lost her baby while we were crossing the mountains."

"Teal, I wish I could help you."

"Only God could do that, and He hasn't. Come with me and meet the others."

He went with her to the next lodge. Seated on scattered bedding, three men and a woman looked up at him, their faces so inscrutable that he felt a ripple of apprehension up his back. None made acknowledgment as Teal, nodding from one to the other, ticked them off.

"Running Wolf and Ten Owl are my brothers. Lone Bird is my sister, and Swift Water is her husband. They obviously aren't pleased that you're here, in spite of my explanation. The young people trust nothing, and they fear my white blood might have blinded me to your intentions."

"Tell them I share their doubts. It would be a bad mistake to figure the trouble's over until there's been a powwow with the Army. The settlers don't have the power to make treaties."

Running Wolf was the largest of the men, obviously the family head. He spoke quickly, and Teal turned again to Kelsey. "You've got a chance to reassure him if you know whether Howard is following us across the mountains and are willing to tell."

He shook his head. "I honestly don't know, Teal. But it's best to figure that he is and to remember there are many more soldiers at Shaw and Benton, and on east at Keogh, in the direction you're heading for buffalo." As he talked, pity for these pure-blooded ones hit him deeply.

The time passed much more swiftly than Kelsey had expected. Once he had been accepted by Teal's people, thoroughly probed and cunningly tested, they began to lose something of their reserve. He was not harangued, and the talk moved to the lesser affairs of life and the buffalo hunt on which they hoped they would soon be embarked. In the last analysis, they asked not for redress of all the long list of wrongs against them, but to be let alone in a fair degree of freedom. He had known few white men who would not fight to the death for the same thing.

At last, when he was bedded down to sleep with men who so shortly back he had fought against in White Bird Canyon, an unwonted exhilaration rose to fill him. His mind went back to what Trace had said to him about the wildness in his blood that he needed to curb. Trace had been right about its presence. The essential nature of a man never rested until he let it find expression, and the avenues of expression could be a surprise even to himself.

CHAPTER NINE

I T was in the small of the morning that he heard it, somewhere short of dawn. A gun, and then another, shattered the stillness of the night. Then came four shots strung together, all from the west.

He threw back the covering of his bed and sat up, seeing the dark figures of Teal's brothers scramble up. Excited cries passed between them, unintelligible to Kelsey, and these were drowned by three volleys from massed rifles and an outbreak of distant shouts. Running Wolf and the others were tugging on their moccasins, then they swept up weapons and darted forth into the dark.

Stunned and completely bewildered, Kelsey knew he had been caught in a surprise attack on the camp. He had pulled on his boots in mechanical urgency, and as he rose up he seized his pistol. He settled it in his holster, understanding in a sickening exposure of realities that he was trapped where he could fight neither red man nor white.

The spaces of the village gave up the sound of swift, soft running. Cries tossed about, of warning, of alarm and despair. The shooting and more distant shouting drew nearer, and he heard bullets rip through the walls of the tepee. He ducked outside to see men and women lying flat on the ground, staring into the darkness where the slant across the river climbed to the timber above. The assault was coming down that slope, the opening shots having dealt with the Indian outguard.

Now nothing stood between the attackers and the village, its women, its old, and its very young.

Not again, he thought. Good God, not again!

The answer was the outburst of a Gatling gun set up on the slope, which told him this was the regular Army, somehow having slipped up in force in the night. Mechanical and firing automatically, the Gatling threw its slugs into the village. The mounting supporting fire drew nearer, scarcely answered as yet because of the milling turmoil in the camp.

He ducked into Teal's tepee, heard a muffled cry, and hastily identified himself. "It's Kelsey. Get out of here, Teal—all of you!"

"My sister—we can't move her!" Teal's voice was a torn wail.

"I'll carry her."

"But where?"

He had no real answer, for where could these people run, ever, to be safe? Rage rose in him, eating at his restraints, inflamed by that hail of lead against these homes. Wailing and sharp outcries all about told him that the toll of dead and hurt already was mounting. But the closer, defensive shooting was growing a little heavier, too.

Coming closer, Teal clutched his arms, staring at him. "But you'd better try to slip away. I don't know what my people will think now. Maybe that you managed to signal somebody that we were off guard. Go now, please."

"No."

He tried to think, picturing the layout of the camp

and its surroundings as he had casually observed them coming in. The village was on a bend of the river, at the edge of a flat. There was no shelter anywhere except in the dubious concealment of the banks and brush downstream.

He said, "Stay with your mother, and I'll try to keep up. Cut to the back side of the village, then go left down the creek. Try to find cover down there. They'll rush this camp in a minute, and kill everything they see."

He dropped to his knees beside the sick girl and in that instant knew that it was already too late. The warning shouts of Indians gave way to a bristling outburst of defensive fire. Somewhere close at hand, soldiers were trying to cross the river, which he knew could be waded almost anywhere. He rose and sprinted out, calling, "Keep down!"

Dawn had begun to dissolve the darkness, and he saw that the blue-shirted attackers were pouring across the upper village, a sprinkling of civilian volunteers mixed in. A far greater force supported them and was stretched along the full front of the camp. Warriors rose up to meet the pioneers over in splashing rushes. Abruptly it was a hot, mixed-up fight, and he kept his place at the tepee door, determined to defend it with his life, pressed flat to the ground.

Warriors came running along the line of tepees toward the hand-to-hand struggle. Between him and the river lay a woman without life. A baby lay on her breast, and it slowly waved an arm from which dangled a bloody hand held only by a shred of flesh. At the edge of the water was the body of a half-grown boy, shot to death.

Smoke was rising in the upper village as lodges were fired without regard for what was caught within. Reinforcements kept pressing across the river, and he saw a trooper fall in the water and begin to float downstream. He saw a volunteer swing a clubbed rifle against the head of an old man. The flames mixed their sound with the drumming shots and steady yelling, while smoke of fires and gunpowder cut into the dust. Maybe a hundred had got over, he estimated, with an undetermined number trying to cross.

All down the stream guns still poured a hail of bullets into the parts of the village not yet penetrated by the assault. He knew that some of the noncombatants had escaped downstream, but also that the majority of them were in the tepees or runways, pressed hard to the earth and dependent on the comparative few who could defend them.

As the close fighting boiled ever hotter, he knew that the camp was doomed. He turned to call to Teal that their only chance lay in running for it, whatever the odds, and his moving glance froze on a point across and a little down from him.

A man whose wet clothing tagged him as a volunteer rose up from the brush, turned, and motioned to the rear. A new crossing was starting here. Grimly Kelsey swung the sights of his revolver, regretting it but without choice. Yet the man fell before he had triggered, cut down by some unseen Indian gun. Then, as volunteers boiled out at him, something exploded violently inside his head and he felt himself going into a helpless forward pitch. He was not aware of even hitting the ground. . . .

When he recovered he was in brush and all alone, while pain made a mute roaring in his head through which drifted the sound of continued but more distant fighting. His clothes were wet. He remembered the volunteer assault he had started to meet and wondered if one of them, mistaking him for one of their own, had dragged him to safety. But he apparently was across the river from the village, and this puzzled him.

His head was bloody all along one temple, and the flow had come down over his face on the upturned cheek. Then he remembered Teal, her mother and helpless sister, and tried to get up. He couldn't make it at first, sagging back in dizzy sickness. Despair hit him as he saw in his mind the surge of white men boiling out of the brush at that part of the village just before he went down.

He crawled forward and again lay still, for directly below him in the water were several Indian women and children, submerged and frightened, with only their heads above the surface. He saw from the pocking of the water that someone was shooting at them from a point upstream. Abruptly a head canted, the face relaxing, then one of the women floated downstream as the water grew red about her.

From this changed position he could see the stark remains of the village, many of its tepees now smoking ashes. But the fighting had cleared out. When at last he got to an unsteady stand against the sheltering trunk of a willow, he could see that the fighting there was through. The fire pattern, still heavy and insistent, conveyed to him that the raiders had been driven out of the village before its total destruction had been accomplished.

He was weak, too spent as yet to do more than stand there. The curve in the slant behind him cut the present phase of the battle from sight, although sharpshooters were scattered close on this side to harry the refugees from the encampment. He saw no place where he could get back over without being fired upon from both sides, but he had to find out about Teal.

He began to work his way upstream, slowly probing and crawling through the undergrowth. He knew that as long as he remained on this side of the river he was in little danger from the assault force, for his clothes would tag and save him. He had covered only a little ground when sudden shouting came from ahead. He recognized Nez Percé voices. He crawled to the edge of the thicket, rose up a little with a thin screen before him, and let his mouth drop open.

Regular and volunteer, the white forces were in open retreat up the wide reach of the slope, running, halting to shoot, then whirling on toward a wooded flat at the top. The jubilant cries of the Indians harried them as much as the searching bullets and arrows. He saw men of his own race stagger and fall and was without pity. They had been brave and steady men in the attack on the sleeping encampment. Now they ran because they were getting back as hot and heavy as they had sent.

The retreat was quickly over, the soldiery reaching

the higher timber and forming there to re-entrench. Return fire speedily stopped the relentless pursuit, the warriors melting into clumps of brush. A new crescendo came in the shooting, but there was gain, Kelsey thought. The battle had moved beyond rifle reach of the village. The Indians had pinned it down up there, swiftly getting around the woods. Kelsey settled down where he was and sank once more into a dizzy, drowsy inertia.

He was aroused by someone's hand shaking him, and he looked up into the slack, spent face of Teal. His first question was: "Your folks?" but she only shook her head. He saw that she was wet from crossing the river and had brought materials to bind his wound.

"Are you all right?" he insisted.

"I'm not hit," she said, and her eyes were a thousand years old.

"How did I get here?"

"I brought you over. It was an Indian who shot you. I saw it."

"But the whites—I saw them coming."

"They shot my mother and burned our tepee and my sister with it. I'd pulled you into the brush, or they would have killed me. I brought you on across because my people will kill you, now, if they find you. Do you feel strong enough to ride and get away? I'll try to bring you a horse."

"I won't leave you."

"You can do no good. My brothers are still alive. I saw them. And I have buried our dead." Swift hands were already at work on his wound. She said, "The horses were shot or scattered, the white men's with them. The soldiers can't get away. But our warriors captured a volunteer who said they are under Gibbon. Howard is close with reinforcements, and there are more volunteers coming from Virginia City."

"Oh, God. Isn't there any end?"

"Yes. And a great many of us came to it, this morning. But Joseph has told us to break camp and go on. Our warriors will stay to keep the soldiers from following us. But you must go because I will now worry about you as you have about me."

"Why, Teal?"

She only shook her head, then slipped off into the undergrowth.

The fighting up above had quieted, and the position of the bald and burning sun told him that it was still morning. Yet it seemed an eternity to him since he had awakened to the first punching shot.

He tried to understand the Army and the volunteers and could not. Colonel Gibbon had completely disregarded an actual *status quo* of peace and had stealthily, brutally pressed on for this attack. The action seemed incredibly stupid, if nothing else, for again the Army had come off whipped, and no longer would the Nez Percés cling to their nonbelligerent attitude toward the settlers. The man had set Montana on fire in wanton willfulness, another soldier hungry for glory or pushed on by blind arrogance in Washington.

Teal returned to him quietly. She said, "I left a horse for you in the brush, on this side, far down the river. There's nobody between. Move quietly and ride through the woods until you're well away. Now, Kelsey. I've got to get ready to leave, and I want to know that you're safe."

Regarding her, he knew that his feeling for her was intimate and personal and very deep. It was different from anything he had ever felt before for a woman, far more selfless than his passion for Glenna. Something in that deep nerve in a man that tells him the truth made plain to him that she returned it in kind, felt it now in spite of her great shock and sorrow.

He said, "I want to go with you."

"You can't. Your life—everything. You've seen our side of it but that doesn't change anything except your attitude. So leave, and God keep you."

"And you, then. So long."

"Good-by."

He turned into the undergrowth, unseeing and uncaring about his own escape except that she wanted it so. That bit of comfort was all he could give her ever and a hundredfold less than what he wanted to give.

CHAPTER TEN

H E rode up to the Buckmaster freightyard with admitted reluctance. Somehow it was with a sense of obligation, as well, and the feeling that what he must say could result in nothing but trouble. He might have lied, claiming his wound had been inflicted upon him by stray Indians he had jumped on the lonely trail, and no one would be able to dispute it. But he had committed himself to the course of truth back at the ranch, where he had arrived just after midnight. He had made a frank account of his injury and of the horse he had forked on an Indian saddle.

Trace was at his desk and shot up a shocked stare as Kelsey walked in.

Kelsey said, "Where's Glenna?"

"Dressmaker's. What in hell happened to you?"

"I was at the Big Hole. You hear about that?"

"I ain't heard much else this morning. Man, you're quick getting in on them scraps. You're going to get killed the next time."

"I didn't do any fighting. Visited the camp and got caught when it was jumped."

"Wait a minute," Trace said, and rose from the desk. "What're you trying to give me, boy?"

"The straight goods. There's a niece of Johnny Hite's. A half-blood. She's with the Nez Percés. When I got to Ross Hole, I decided to drop over the pass, check up on her, then come on home that way."

"Slept there, did you? Must have, or you wouldn't of got caught."

Kelsey felt his neck redden. "That's right. Alone."

"Well, I don't reckon I'd tell Glenna. Been hard on her having you gone and her trying to get ready for the wedding."

"Time for her to start worrying about me is when I start lying to her."

"Me, I don't blame a man for foxing around a little. Used to, myself. But right on top of getting married—" Trace shook his head. "Look. Some bucks took horses away from you in Ross Hole. She'd swallow that."

Kelsey shrugged, feeling no inclination to argue the point. "What's the story on the fracas?" he asked.

Apparently Trace thought that his daughter was going to be spared the painful truth. Easing visibly, he said, "As bad a bungling job as has been pulled yet. Howard come up to relieve Gibbon, who didn't need it by the time he got there. The Injuns just pulled stakes. A half-done thing again. Them Nez Percés lost most of their horses and supplies. They'll have to find more in the field, and they'll take 'em where they find 'em. The governor's mobilizing the militia in full strength. There ain't a town or ranch on the upper Missouri that'll be safe till them sonsabitches are all killed off."

"Thought you wanted a man-size war—same as Halverson."

"I never said so."

"Neither did he. I'm going to the doctor, Trace. If you see Glenna, tell her I'm in town."

"Don't forget you lost horses to the Injuns. I'll back your story."

The wound needed cleaning, suturing, and rebinding, so it was quite a while before Kelsey left the doctor's inner office and walked out into the bare reception room. Glenna rose out of a chair, her face blanched.

She cried, "Kelsey! Dad just told me! How awful!" Her shocked anxiety was so real, so deep, that he could not ask her immediately just what she had been told. He took her in his arms and felt her trembling.

"All fixed," he told her. "And Doc says no brains leaked out."

"You might have been killed!" she wailed. "Drat you, you've got to keep away from where they're fighting!"

"Ready to go home?"

"Yes."

"How's the wedding dress?"

"Coming along. Darling, I got so scared I'm still sick."

So he said nothing as they emerged to the sidewalk and started home together. He led his horse, meaning to head out of town as soon as he could. Then, as the shock wore off, she thought of the things he dreaded to discuss.

"But tell me about it," she said. "How many Indians were there, and did you kill any?"

"Looks like your dad told you a windy about me losing horses to the Nez Percés."

"Why, didn't you?"

"No. And Trace knows better. When I got to Ross Hole, I was close to the Indian camp. So—"

"So you went to see Teal Shannon again?"

"Yes."

"Oh, you didn't! You didn't!"

"I told Trace so. But since I got caught there in bed, he put the wrong light on it, and figured you would too."

"In bed? Why on earth—"

"Look," he said. "Try to remember I could have let

102

Trace's yarn ride, and it would have been easier on us both. I don't like to do business with you that way, Glenna, not now or ever. What I did was on impulse and anything but smart. The Nez Percés wouldn't let me go till they were ready to break camp for fear I was a spy. That's what they still thought after Gibbon barreled in on 'em—that I managed to signal that they were off guard. It was an Indian that shot me, all right, if that makes you feel any better."

"Was she killed?"

"Her mother and sister were. She saved my life and got me a horse to get away on. I'm grateful. Since I was fool enough to go there, it seems to me you ought to appreciate it, too."

"Oh, I do," Glenna said in quick contrition. "But I just can't understand it, Kelsey."

"Rather I'd lied?"

"Yes, because I never even suspected the truth."

She shrugged, and they walked in silence until they reached her porch. Her face was a clear mirror of the things at war within her. When she opened the door and waited for him to enter, he shook his head.

"I got to get on home. They fixed that place up real fancy while I was gone. You be out pretty soon?"

"Of course."

"You're not sore at me?"

"Since you admire the truth so much, I am. You're interested in that girl. More than you let on, or else more than you know."

"She's in a hell of a fix."

"Sympathy's got sharp hooks on it, darling."

Smiling suddenly, she added in quick serenity, "I'm not going to rawhide you about it. I've been happy getting things ready. There's so much to do."

"Been able to set the date?"

"Not exactly. But it'll probably be the end of the month."

Kelsey returned to the ranch with a strong desire to plunge into work so he could keep his mind off a new crop of gnawing, unsettled notions in the indistinct depths of his mind. The ferment he had thought ended by the plans for his union with Glenna was a thing he hated to look at again.

The horses he had bought on his circuit down the valleys had in most part been brought to the ranch. Many of them were already broken to pack. Others only needed finishing off, while a few were plain green. With regular work in addition, he was soon submerged and able to sleep at nights. His wound was clean and healing rapidly, although he knew that Big Hole had put a different kind of mark on him that would linger long.

In his absence, workmen had been at the ranch, and Kelsey guessed it had been quite a crew. There was now water in the house, coming from a windmill and cistern, while the kitchen had been built over completely. And yet somehow the thought of Glenna's arrival at the ranch to live with him had lost a part of its savor.

He had known that he and Glenna were not in perfect harmony, but he had assumed that to be so in most cases. Now he knew what rightness could be, knew it too late, knew it with resignation. He had pressed too hard for Glenna to pull back from his own choosing.

He put in two weeks of unbroken labor, not visiting the town. He saw Glenna only when she found time to come out and spend a few hours. She was as affectionate as ever; it was he who began to withdraw into himself, until at last she said, "You've got so much on your mind there isn't room for me, is there?"

"Fiddlesticks," he snapped, and realized at once that his voice had been too vehement to reassure her.

"Touchy about it, too," she reflected. "I haven't much hold on you, have I? I could lose you pretty easy. If I'm going to, Kelsey, I'd rather have it happen now."

"Look," he said with restored patience. "You're sore about the Big Hole and still suspicious. If I was wrong in going there, I've paid for it. Not only through this sore head of mine, but in the things I remember. Dead kids, dead women, dead old men. It's scrambled my puzzle good."

"And my place in it, unfortunately."

"Keep saying that, and I'll start to believe it."

"Then I'll shut up, because you believe it too much already."

Thereafter she had no sweet and secret side to show him, though outwardly she remained amiable, cheerful, and increasingly excited about the wedding. She set the date, at last, for the twenty-second of August, which by then was so close that Kelsey began to get a bridegroom's stage fright.

Meanwhile he learned something of the Nez Percés'

progress since pulling out of the Big Hole. As was to be expected, they had picked up horses and supplies where they found them. On Birch Creek they had captured a freight train bound for the town of Salmon, killing three white men in the fight and losing none themselves. The Indians were reported to be heading for Targhee Pass, toward the new national park on the headwaters of the Yellowstone. Howard and his tired foot soldiers slogged patiently behind.

Then came another summons from Trace. Irritated at the interruption and dreading what might be asked of him again, Kelsey saddled and went in to town. His feelings were not improved when he walked into Trace's office to find Lafe Halverson there.

The man merely nodded, and it was all too plain that he remembered the bald charges made against him in Lewiston.

"You're a long ways from home, man," Kelsey said.

Halverson shrugged.

"He's got news," Trace said. "And a job for you."

"I'm not working for him."

"You're working for me, by God, and we agreed you'd take my orders as long as that was the case. Something happened that would be funny if it wasn't so goddamn critical. The Injuns took Howard's pack mules away from him. He's stalled up at Henry's Lake. Was about out of supplies already. Told you I was smart when I set you to buying horses. You're going to take him a new pack train loaded with stores from here."

"He know I am?" Kelsey asked.

Trace nodded. "Lafe arranged it. Hell of a note, sending you out again with the wedding so near, but it can't be helped. With the best of it, Howard ain't come within shooting distance of them siwashes since the Clearwater fight. With him bogged down, they're going to have a free hand."

Kelsey could not see Halverson except as a cunning, covetous, and wholly unscrupled man. It filled him with distaste to lend himself even in part to the man's use. But what Trace had said about the situation was right. Besides, he felt sympathy for the worn, ragged infantrymen who had come all the way from Fort Lapwai. Not only had they been marched to death; they had been beaten by bad generalship every time they had made contact with their enemies.

And there was more. For some undivined reason, he was nowhere near as disappointed at having the wedding postponed as Trace seemed to be. There was an odd sense of respite in the delay.

"When do I go?" he asked, and that was his decision and assent.

Trace looked relieved. "Soon as you can. We're lining up the stuff to take. You get your string here bright and early in the morning. A hundred horses. Can you scare up enough pack saddles? Bring what you can from the ranch, and I'll try to borrow more around town."

"*You* can tell Glenna that the wedding's postponed," Kelsey said, and walked out.

Kelsey's riders were brothers, Virg and Olney Miller, and the three of them roped out horses for the long pack. They were checking a stack of wooden aparejos that evening when Trace rode in, looking pleased at what he found.

"Who you going to take along?" Trace asked.

Nodding, Kelsey said, "Virg there, and Jimmy Dyke from the yard. You better send Lonzo out here to help Olney."

"Come over to the house," Trace said.

When they reached the porch, Kelsey said, "Let me tell you something again, Trace. I think Lafe Halverson's a low-down son-of-a-bitch, and he knows I do. I don't like you teaming up with him."

"Is that a fact?" Trace said. "You haven't got anything on Lafe."

"He's Johnny on the spot when there's a chance to turn a nickel."

"Neither of us would be where we are if we hadn't been smart. Smart enough to watch what shapes up and see what's to come of it, and then get ready to handle it."

"What's coming this trip, Trace?"

Trace's guess was prompt. "War, the way Lafe says. He's been talking to some treaty Nez Percés back in Idaho—men who know Joseph's mind. They say he'll try to reach the Crows, figuring they'll help him fight the Army. They owe it. You recall how the Nez Percés pulled their fat out of the fire. That was two-three years back, when the Crows fought the Sioux on Prior Creek. Gratis help, it was. The Nez Percés were only over there to make buffalo meat."

"According to Lafe's game of checkers," Kelsey

drawled, "what happens if they get that help?"

"Then," Trace said emphatically, "hell wouldn't have this country. Sitting Bull will skallyhoot down with all the Sioux he took with him after they done for Custer. They been waiting all this time for a chance like that. Given that encouragement, the Blackfeet will jump in, too. Don't look at me that way. I'd stop it if I could. Since I can't, I'm going to give the Army all the help I can."

"And make a profit at it."

"Who don't, when they can?"

CHAPTER ELEVEN

THE pack string camped the second night along the stage road south of Virginia City. The next morning it was near the forks where the pack trail would strike for the Madison Valley and a slow climb to the high plateaus that sheltered Henry's Lake and Howard's stalled infantry.

When the Salt Lake stage came rattling down the grade toward them, a whistle from Virg Miller was enough to turn the string off the road so the Concord could barrel past. But to Kelsey's surprise, the stage driver gave him a quick second look and pulled to a grinding stop, dust enveloping the outfit as Kelsey swung his horse about.

"Buckmaster string, ain't you?" the driver bawled. "Man, I got news for you! One of your wagon outfits is up the road. I aimed to send somebody out from Virginia, but you can take over right here."

The strained faces of passengers staring out at him stirred dread in Kelsey. "What's wrong with it?" he asked.

"Every man's dead, that's all that's wrong!" The driver turned his head to aim tobacco juice at the ground. "Shot and scalped. The redskins tried to burn the wagons, but it didn't work. But they took some stuff and the horses."

"Indians?"

"Who else lifts hair around here?"

"All right. They've got volunteers in Virginia. Tell the captain."

"Right." A whip cracked, and the Concord rolled on.

The three men with the pack train stared at each other through a long moment. "God," Jimmy Dyke said finally.

"Well, you men head on for the Madison," Kelsey said. "I'll go on up the stage road and see, then swing back and catch up. Not that I can do anything." He swung his horse and rode out, moving quietly ahead of the train, then lifting the animal's gait to a steady gallop.

He passed the fork in the road, keeping right. Not long afterward he could see the shapes of stalled wagons in the distance. He slowed his horse, dreading what he would find. The lead wagon stood in the middle of the road, tongue dropped, and the stage had been obliged to pull around it. Then he came upon them, the bodies of three men.

They were sprawled about, without guns, and he saw no empty shells to indicate that they had been able to put up a scrap. A rock scab that skirted the trail explained that. They had been ambushed.

Charred canvas and the scorched sides of the wagons showed that a hurried effort had been made to burn the outfit. All of the three tandem wagons had been ransacked, some of the freight thrown to the ground. He couldn't see where the Indians could have taken very much besides the horses. Swinging from the saddle, he made a careful investigation. At last he rolled a cigarette and smoked it in deep thought. He had made a puzzling discovery.

No freight outfit ever came up from the railroad without a substantial consignment of whisky aboard. At the end of one of the wagons the dust showed imprints where a number of kegs had been dumped out. But now there were no kegs in sight.

The Indians went for firewater when they could get it, but he doubted that they would have attacked a freight train this close to the settlement just for that. At the most they would have bashed in a keg end and satisfied their thirst on the spot. They must have had pack animals along, but it was wholly illogical that they would have packed off what must have been a dozen kegs of whisky. They would have taken food, clothing, and other items for which their need was desperate.

That much whisky would be hard to come by even for a white man, Kelsey thought as he stood lost in wonder; it could not be bought without arousing considerable curiosity. And his jaw muscles slowly bulged as he began to discern a possible use for it. According to what Halverson had told Trace, Chief Joseph hoped to get help from the Crows, whose reservation lay directly east of this point. Maybe Joseph was sending emissaries with gifts of firewater to see that he roused the necessary fighting zeal and support on the reservation.

A little more scouting, and Kelsey was convinced that he had guessed shrewdly. Empty rifle shells showed that three men had lain in ambush in the scab rock. He found tracks where around a dozen horses had come down from the brush above the trail to be loaded. Circling, he picked up sign where an increased band of horses had been ridden or driven on an abrupt angle into the higher hills. He rode the trail a way, trying to fix the direction of travel. It was east, toward the distant Crow reservation. That ended his last doubts.

Just before he was ready to turn back, he made a final discovery. He had come to a point where the raiding party seemed to have separated. One group struck north into more tangled country. That puzzled him, and he decided to follow the sign a way. Presently, topping a rise that gave onto a thickly saged slope, he saw loose horses wearing the Buckmaster brand. They apparently had been left where they were not likely to be found. That was a strange thing to do. For an Indian, the prime prize of war was a good horse. He certainly would not discard a dozen fine ones right out of the best Buckmaster stock. Maybe they had been cached here to be picked up later, but an Indian would know this would become dangerous country to revisit.

Returning to the tragedy at the stalled wagons, Kelsey covered the bodies with pieces of salvaged canvas, then he rose again to leather. He scanned the ground once again, hunting for footprints, but somebody seemed to have brushed out any that had been left accidentally in the dust of the road. That also seemed odd, he thought, as he set out to overtake his packers. What Indian would care about a moccasin imprint when he had put his trademark on the deed by lifting scalps?

Virg and Jimmy had reached the valley of the Madison and turned south toward the headwaters of the river. It was wide, swelling parkland running between mountain rises. The deep green Tobacco Roots rose on the right, and on the other hand ran the blue-tipped Madison Mountains. The ascent was gradual through the sage-brushed foothills.

His packers sighted him in the distance and let the string plod on while they pulled down their own mounts to wait.

"Who was it?" Virg called, his voice filled with apprehension.

Kelsey said, "Ed Hunkel and Mike Nebo and Ridge Dunway. Bushed and likely never knew what hit them. Indians after firewater, from the looks of it, or white men after the same. Near as I could tell, that was about all that was taken. I've got a mighty sick hunch they're packing it in to the Crows, boys. If they get there with it, all hell will bust loose. If I'm right, we ought to pick up sign where they cross the Madison."

"If they do," said Jimmy, "I hope they get it done

long before we come along."

Midafternoon had come before fresh horse droppings gave Kelsey the tip he had hunted all along the way.

He said, "Look, boys. Somebody's got to tell the Indian agent so he can intercept that run of booze. You fellows go on."

"You going to the Crow agency?" Virg asked. "Man, that's a long and lonesome ride."

"I can cut across to Cooke City from here," Kelsey said, "and send somebody on from there. If that whisky ever wets Crow throats, this whole edge of the country will blow sky-high."

"You go trailing that raiding party, and you'll never be around to see that happen," Virg returned.

"I can travel faster than their pack string, son."

Kelsey did not tell them he had no intention of going as far as Cooke City if he could catch that pack string short of there. He thought he knew already the route the raiders would take to reach the Crow reservation with the least chance of being discovered.

It was not hard to cross to the upper Gallatin, whence ran a trail that swung over to the Yellowstone headwaters. The raiding party would almost have to use it. By outriding them, he might be able to get ahead and cut them off. He believed the party to consist of no more than three men, and he accepted those odds.

Against the chance that his mission would take longer than he anticipated, he stowed enough food in his saddlebags to last him a camp or two. In the most casual manner he could manage, he said, "So long. Do your job and go home. If it works out right, I might join up with you. But don't worry about me if I don't." Then he swung off toward the river to cross where the raiders had.

The sign left by so many loaded horses was dead easy to follow. Their drivers seemed to depend on speed to lose them in the rough country instead of trying to foul trail. But he knew they would be watching their back trail as best they could. So when he was certain they meant to cross to the Gallatin, he cut right.

The Gallatin River carved a rugged canyon between the Gallatin and Madison Mountains, confining travelers to a predictable route. In the deep of evening he came down on the trail that ran south and west to the westward pass. Tired as he was, he felt a thrill of elation when he could detect no fresh signs of massed horse travel. If he was right at all, he was ahead of his quarry. But this was not the place to make his challenge, and he pressed on to where the country began to flatten out and widen.

He found a point where they could not yet leave the trail to start skulking again, and there he posted himself to wait. It was getting toward time to camp, but he doubted that they would halt until they were in more open country where they would be safer. So he concealed his horse at a safe distance and, carrying his carbine, returned to take post atop a low bluff.

Idle yet naggingly restless, he could not help facing at last the bitter irony of his being there in that wild and lonely land. Somewhere in the same general vicinity were Teal and her hunted people, hoping for escape, for help, for simple freedom. He would help her if he could, and the Crows might help if they were given enough of the contraband whisky he sought to intercept. Yet in good conscience he could do no less than he was doing. He expected to make a bitter fight against her cause, and he had no choice at all.

The sighing of the pines, the smells of raw nature, the feel of hard warm ground under his belly—all began to stir in him the wild delight he could feel only in such places. His mind strayed from Teal to Glenna, making its reluctant comparisons. He knew that however sincere Glenna had been in her determination to live his kind of life, it was not a durable purpose because it had no natural roots. But with her, as with this thing he must do against Teal, he was committed to the course of conscience.

The first soft sound of warning could have come from several sources. A moment passed before he was sure of the rhythmic footfalls of horses beyond the crest on the downward trail. He had his carbine sights lined on that spot as the first horse came over.

It wore a pack saddle to which were lashed canvas-wrapped objects that might or might not be whisky kegs. A second animal followed, then a string of them, and finally three horsemen broke over together. Kelsey's breath caught and held and he did not tighten his trigger finger as he had intended. He was not wholly surprised, and relieved that they were not Nez Percés. Even in the deep dusk he could tell that they were white men, or at least were dressed like whites.

Then he realized that one of them was Chappy Riskin, knew it beyond question. Hastily he revised his plans of swift and total destruction for Riskin and his saddlemates were tools and not the root evil in the situation. The horses looked played out. It was ten to one that Riskin would soon make camp now that he was out in open country. Kelsey let them trail past his point of vantage unmolested, aware that he would never again have so good a chance at them. But he had to take one of them a prisoner who could talk to the authorities about this and other matters. Soon they had vanished into the trees and the twilight.

He waited for fifteen minutes before he retreated down the shallow ground saddle to the place where he had hidden his horse. Rising up into the saddle, he fished bread and cold meat from a saddle pouch and ate leisurely, giving Riskin time to pick out a campsite and set up. He allowed himself the comfort of a quick smoke, then moved out along a course parallel to the trail.

He had gone better than a mile when he saw the distant glimmer of a fire. He halted at once and swung down to wait again. Night had deepened, and now and then he could see some shape outline itself in silhouette against the blaze. They would be hungry men, off guard when they had begun to eat. He would give them time to get supper ready.

It was not easy to linger there, waiting and weighing his chances. They seemed to take forever with the cooking.

The horses were on the grass under the pines, too far away to betray him with a show of interest. The freight packs were heaped to his right. When he saw the men begin to hunker down with their tin plates, Kelsey silently moved to bring the packs between himself and the fire. Then he began to go in.

He crawled the last distance, his breath flowing soft and shallow from his lungs. He had to be sure of one thing before he made his deadly challenge. When he reached the edge of the freight heap, a searching hand on the hard outline of a keg confirmed his suspicion. He quietly rose, his revolver a little high, then chopping down. His voice punched into the talkless silence of hungry men feeding.

"Don't move a thing but your arms, and shove them high!"

He had them dead to rights, but there were three of them. The youngest of the lot so closely resembled Chappy Riskin that he had to be the renegade Billy. This was the one in whom brashness boiled over. He twisted, taking a desperate chance on reaching his gun in time. As Kelsey shot, Ben and Chappy both bolted for the weaker light. Kelsey flattened Ben, but Chappy seemed simply to melt into the combination of night and high grass. Afraid to empty his gun, Kelsey did not riddle the point at which the man had vanished. All he could do was pull back into full concealment himself.

When he had retreated some twenty yards from the pack heap, he began to circle to the right. He knew he had hit Ben and could hardly have missed Billy, but that did not mean they were out of the fight. After the rocking roar of his gun, the forest seemed deathly quiet. Presently he could see into the camp and detect the still shapes on the ground there. Those two men were either dead, badly hit, or playing possum. Until he could find out which, they were as dangerous as if fully able-bodied. But the most dangerous one was Chappy, whom he had lost in the night.

By taking a chance himself, he might get Chappy to betray his position. Kelsey weighed it through a tense moment, then called out, "Riskin!"

Chappy did not take the bait, and Kelsey frowned, aware that time ran against him. But he did not try to trick Riskin again. The man was betting on a waiting game to put the whisky, for which he had murdered three freighters, back into his own possession.

Then, out of the great stillness, came the sudden swift drum of hoofs. Stunned by his disbelief in Riskin's willingness to abandon the contraband so readily, Kelsey stared into the blackness. A cold grin built itself momentarily on his mouth. Maybe the renegade had a few tricks up his own sleeve.

Dropping flat to the belly, he again began a patient crawl toward the heaped packs. He reached them without contest and there removed his hat. He bent the brim for a grip and very slowly pushed the crown up into the stronger light of the fire. A rifle cracked in instant, vicious response.

He let pass the first seconds Chappy took to jack in a fresh cartridge and again shoot at the hat. That shot tore the hat from his grip, but he was springing to his feet. He shot at the point he had fixed, a split second before he yelled.

"Man can use a hat for more than slapping a horse's rump, Chappy!"

Then he shot twice more.

Again the return was silence and the bewildered tension of not knowing what toll he had taken and of not daring to risk his life again to find out. Once more forted in the concealment of the packs, he realized that the balance could swing against him as easily as against his enemy. He had to destroy this whisky before he did anything else. Then, no matter what the outcome, it could not serve its intended purpose.

Once more he crawled, this time working directly away from the camp and toward the place where he had left his horse. He had not brought his carbine for the close shooting, and now he wanted it. When he reached the horse, he pulled the carbine from the boot. He picked out a pine bole that would protect him, figuring he had a little time before Chappy could work around and get in behind him. He began to send the carbine's drilling slugs into the wrapped kegs. At the same time he closely watched the environs for a softer target.

Although Riskin must have realized that his precious whisky was being soaked up by the thirsty earth, he lacked the courage to make a contesting fire. But Kelsey knew that the man was not idle, that he was trying to gain an advantageous position. Kelsey emptied the carbine, trying to hit the kegs as near the ground as possible.

He dared not take time to reload the weapon, and he let it drop, instantly drawing his pistol. Now he wanted Riskin, wanted him alive. After this evidence of whisky running, the authorities would wring the truth from the man somehow, find out who backed him. Kelsey stood where he was, since Riskin would expect him to change place. He was so tight with tension that his whole body ached from it.

CHAPTER TWELVE

H^E could see the campfire, which no one had been able to scatter, and suddenly he wondered if he had not misguessed Riskin's present activity. Were the situation reversed, he knew what he would be doing now. He would try to see how badly hurt his brother was; he would put that above every other consideration.

Therefore he quietly placed himself where, if Riskin tried to crawl in to the edge of the firelight, he would have to outline himself a little against it. He had not much hope, for the things he had seen bearing the Riskin signature denied the man's possession of many such tender feelings.

But suddenly he had the merest impression of movement between himself and the fire. He tensed, his eyes trying to probe the dark. The effort was fruitless, yet some instinct told him that Riskin was between him and the camp.

Kelsey started forward, lowering each step with patience, exploring for a twig that might snap, settling his feet slowly and gently upon centuries of leaf mold on the forest floor. Presently he could see the two sprawled figures on the ground. Again he waited. Hunkering finally, he picked up the rounded black outlines of something cutting off part of the light. It could be a rock, or it could be a man.

He gambled everything. Softly he called, "I've got my gun on you, Riskin. Stand up or I'll drill you. I mean it."

The first sign that he was right came from the fact that no gun spat at him from another position. The outline he watched did not move, and he started on in. Then all at once the shape vanished, and he shot reluctantly, running forward as the crash of the explosion shattered the forest. Then Riskin shoved up into plain view, yelling.

"All right. All right!" He dropped his gun.

"Step over into the firelight, Riskin. Quick!"

Riskin responded by trotting to Billy and dropping down on his knees. He lowered his head and placed his ear on the kid's chest and was like that for a long moment. Kelsey picked up the gun he had dropped.

"I thought he was alive and needed me," Riskin said, straightening, "or I wouldn't of quit. You killed him, Ames. You killed my brother."

"He asked for it, and so did you. Time and again."

"I'll get you for it."

"Then you'll have to come back from hell, because you're going to hang. And I hope Lafe Halverson swings with you."

It was frightening to see the twisted emotion on

Riskin's whiskery features. He seemed dazed, and it was apparent that thought of his own freedom had weighed less with him than his need to make sure about Billy. Now he was thinking of that liberty, and temper scudded through the deep bitterness in his eyes.

"Nobody's going to hang me, man. You or anybody else."

"We're going down to Virginia. But you can take time to bury your saddlemates if you've got a shovel."

"I got no shovel, and we ain't going down to Virginia."

"Look, Riskin," Kelsey said. "I went to some pains to take you alive. Give me trouble now, and I still won't kill you, but I'll put slugs through your legs. Cover Billy and Ben with something. There'll be somebody up here tomorrow, anyhow. Then take that ax and knock the heads in on them kegs. And see you do a good job."

For a moment the renegade seemed on the point of rebellion. But he was squarely covered, and the sand began to run out of him. He covered Ben's body first, then took more pains about it when he got to Billy.

When he had finished, he raked Kelsey with hot eyes. "I ain't going to kill you, either, buck. I'll get somebody you care about. What I hear, there ain't many you do. You and me are kind of alike, that way, mebbe. Wouldn't give two bits for the whole goddamn world, except for one or two."

"So you really cared for Billy."

"All I ever had and the only one who ever give a

123

good goddamn about me. I heard about you getting married, Ames, and I'm telling you. I know how to get you for this."

The impact was like sand blown on raw nerves. Kelsey narrowed his lids. "You're going to hang. But if for some reason you don't, then I'll find and kill you. Quick and easy, unless you give me reason to make it otherwise. Remember that. Now get your ax."

Reluctantly Riskin obeyed. Afterward, when he was certain that his mission was fully accomplished, Kelsey went with him while the man caught his horse and brought it in to saddle up. Then they picked up his own mount and finally were on the descending trail again, Riskin riding ahead with no chance to bolt for it in the narrow stricture of the long canyon.

When he reached Butte, two afternoons later, Kelsey went directly to the Buckmaster freightyard. As he rode through the main gate, he saw the charred wagons that had been brought in from the Corinne road. Trace was standing in the door of the blacksmith shop.

"So you finally got back from your wild-goose chase!" Trace bawled, and Kelsey knew that Virg and Jimmy had returned from Henry's Lake.

Riding on across the yard, Kelsey swung down, tired and at the end of his tolerance. Eying Trace in a slow, detached way, he said, "I've got an idea you'll wish it was only a wild-goose chase, man. Because you're not going to like what I've got to tell you. I killed two Halverson men and I turned the third over to the law at Virginia yesterday. Chappy Riskin."

"Riskin?" Shock stood on Trace's face. "Jimmy said you figured maybe it wasn't Injuns but whisky runners. But what's this talk about Halverson?"

"He's behind it. I've told you two or three different times, Trace. Now three of your own men have been murdered. Halverson might not have ordered it specifically. Maybe he only told Riskin to get hold of whisky somehow and deliver it to the Crows. Just the same, he's an accessory to murder, and I say it's high time you got your eyes open."

"Riskin confess to it?"

"Of course not."

"And he ain't likely going to."

"That what you hope, Trace? Can't you bear to think of giving up what looks like nice new business through Halverson's efforts?"

"Blast it, you're dead wrong about Lafe!" Trace said, and temper swelled his face and neck. "For some reason you took a dislike to him, and you're set on running him down. But it takes more than your say-so to sway my opinion. That plain?"

"Plain enough."

"Then make no more such talk while you're working for me."

"That a threat, Trace?"

"Take it the way you want."

"I aim to see Halverson swing, so I better quit here and now."

"Now, keep your shirt on," Trace said.

Shrugging, Kelsey said, "Glenna home?"

"I reckon so."

Kelsey rose to the saddle, but before riding off he looked down at Trace again. He said, "Understand one thing: I'll do my regular work, but don't try to put me on any more of the new stuff. I won't have any part of it. The minute you try to crowd me into it, I'll take your precious daughter into the prairie and set up in business for myself."

Trace's thick shoulders slowly lifted and slowly fell. Then he turned into the blacksmith shop.

A night's sleep at the ranch restored Kelsey physically but did nothing to relieve the returned tension in his mind. He wasn't lifted in spirit when he discovered that Glenna had sent a considerable amount of furniture from the town place to the ranch house. It was all too easy, too far above what would have to be their eventual scale of living. And it was all too much her own doing, at what probably was her father's behest.

Totaling up the concessions he had already made to her, Kelsey realized that he had all but given away piecemeal what he had so steadily refused to yield in a single assent. Such concessions carried their own momentum, quickly snowballing and hard to stop.

I've got to make the break before the wedding, he thought, and not wait till after it's done.

Now he knew that before they even so much as rehearsed the ceremony, he had to talk with Glenna and wring from her an agreement that they would not come here to live but would strike out on their own at once. He had saved enough to do it, and the right kind of woman would want it the same as he did. He had to lay it on the line for her, because he might never again draw a free breath if he accepted all this even temporarily.

But bad news reached the ranch late the next afternoon when Jimmy Dyke came out with a bunch of horses from the town stables. His greeting was terse.

"Well, a lot of good you done yourself in the mountains, Kelsey. Somebody sprung Chappy Riskin out of the Virginia jail."

"You sure?"

"Talked to a man who just come from Virginia," Jimmy said. "Somebody sneaked into the jailhouse and cold-cocked the turnkey. Man never even got a look at the fellow. When he come to, Chappy's cell was unlocked and empty as a percentage gal's heart."

"Riskin's from Idaho," Kelsey breathed. "He doesn't know anybody over here who'd do that for him. Halverson hasn't even had time to hear about his being locked up, much less send anybody over here."

"Who's Halverson?"

"Never mind."

Leaving Jimmy, Kelsey headed for the day corral to get a horse. A cold, compelling suspicion had risen in his mind. The only man on the Montana side of the mountains he had discussed his convictions with was Trace. And Trace had been vehement in his statement that Riskin would never tell anything on Halverson.

Kelsey knew he had to face it, to weigh it coolly. He doubted that Trace had ever actually schemed with Halverson, plotting the incredibly cruel things that had been done to foment Indian trouble. If he had himself freed Riskin or found a man he could trust to do it, he had probably acted out of friendship and his desire to team anew with the man who had such a genius for making money. There was one possible additional motive—a fear that, if Halverson was embroiled in difficulties with the law, he might himself be drawn in because of his known connections with the man.

Kelsey stopped at the house first, when he reached Butte, feeling a need to tell Glenna beforehand that he meant to have a final showdown with her father. He gave her a long and almost critical look.

"What's wrong?" she asked.

"More than I want to look at. I aim to have a talk with Trace. Figured I'd tell you before I went down to the yard."

"No need to go there. He's here taking a nap. He just got home from a trip."

"Trip? Where?"

Glenna shrugged. "Business somewhere. Kelsey, what's up? I've got to know before you see him."

"I'm quitting him. Then, if you want to go downtown and have the justice of the peace marry us up, we'll head east. For keeps."

"When?"

"Tomorrow at the latest."

She looked stricken. "What's got into you? The wedding's tomorrow, anyway! The church is all ready!"

Sighing, he said, "Call Trace. It's really between him and me, anyhow. But maybe you'd better listen in."

He saw stubbornness rise in her features. Turning, she vanished through an inner doorway. Presently Trace padded in with his boots off, sleepy-eyed and tousle-haired. He came alone.

"Must be behind on sleep," Kelsey said.

Frowning, Trace said, "What's this you've been saying that's got Glenna so upset?"

"Long ride to Virginia," Kelsey said, unheeding. "Man wouldn't get a chance to sleep except in the saddle."

"What's that about Virginia?"

"Just got back from there, didn't you?"

"All right, I did. Some things you said wormed into my brain. I wanted to have a talk with Riskin."

"Planning to spring him?" Kelsey asked. "Or did he blackmail you into it when you saw him?"

"I don't know what you're driving at."

"Don't try to fool me, Trace. Riskin's loose, and God help you if you're responsible. There's something I could have told you that might have stopped you. Riskin threatened me. Not personally. He threatened to get at me through somebody I care about."

"But why?"

"I killed Billy. Chappy aims to get back at me through Glenna."

Trace's usually florid cheeks had gone an ashen gray. He made no acknowledgments and never would. Yet his eyes all but confessed his guilt.

"My God," he growled. "We got to get her out of the country for a while."

"Better if Riskin was still in jail."

"You won't believe me," Trace said, "but I never had a thing to do with his getting out. I can read men. I figured I could ask him some questions and find out pretty sure whether Lafe's behind him."

"Did you find out?"

"Yeah. He threatened to pull Lafe and me both into it unless we got him out of there real quick. But I told him I hoped he hanged."

"Come clean, Trace. He scared you so bad that you hired some Virginia City punk to go in there and bring him out."

"When you get a notion," Trace retorted, "you're like a mule. Believe what you damned please."

"All right," Kelsey said tiredly. "I couldn't prove you had a hand in it, and I'm not interested in trying. But are you going on doing business with Halverson?"

"That's my affair."

"All right again. I reckon Glenna told you I'm quitting. I'll go through with her big wedding if she's still set on having it. But only if she'll leave with me afterward. You've loosed the lightning, Trace. If you really want her to get out of the country to escape it, that's how she can do it."

"There's another way," Trace said harshly. "And that's for her to break with you. The better I know you, the more I figure it's past time she done it."

"Then you'd get word to Riskin real quick that he can no longer hurt me through Glenna. You still wouldn't have crossed him so he might drag you into trouble with him. Clever, Trace—and snake-blooded. But I want Glenna to tell me we're through, not you."

Swinging around, Trace walked out of the room.

There was another interval before Glenna reappeared.

"The answer is no," she said.

"It's now or never, Glenna."

"Then it's never. You're utterly unreasonable."

"Obedient to the very last," he said softly.

The stiffness of her body told him everything in their shared past had been destroyed. There was no point in hammering at her that her father was consorting with crooks and worse, condoning them with the same kind of mental dishonesty she herself possessed.

"So long, then."

"You're bound to go?"

"There's no other way. None of the things you promised about our independence has come true. And you never really meant for them to, did you?"

"Maybe not. Because I knew I never really had you. It's been that Indian girl ever since you met her."

"Never mind her. Just you tell Trace to put my check in my account at the bank."

"Kelsey!"

"Hasta la vista."

She whirled and fled through the inner doorway.

CHAPTER THIRTEEN

BOZEMAN was a cow town near the pass out of the upper Missouri Valley, the gateway to the high plains, the free range, and the mustangs on which he must depend for his living until he got started on a breeding ranch of his own. He spent what might have been his wedding night in that town, the next morning pressing on. He had his string of private horses, a pack outfit, and his saddler. He had a sense of ease, of elation beyond anything he had ever known.

He wanted to see Teal, who even now was somewhere in the uplands of the geyser country, interminably in flight. In a Bozeman saloon he had heard that the Nez Percés could not have been far from where he had taken Chappy Riskin into custody.

He had picked up one final bit of news that, while it should have seemed good from a white man's viewpoint, somehow depressed him. Out of Fort Lincoln, Colonel Sturgis had come by steamboat to the mouth of the Big Horn. Kelsey's old outfit, the Seventh Cavalry, was in the field against Joseph. Sturgis was using Crow scouts who, so far, were making the only contact with the Nez Percés—their gratuitous allies against the Sioux—and each time coming off the losers.

So Joseph would not receive the help he hoped for and had come a thousand miles to get. Kelsey's conscience was tinged with a shade of guilt for his own part in preventing such an alliance. With Sturgis ahead and Howard behind, the Nez Percés again seemed caught in a trap from which there could be no escape, whose only outcome would be ruin and ruthless slaughter. He wanted desperately to extricate Teal from the situation even while knowing he could never persuade her to desert her people.

In the mountain pass leading to the Yellowstone sat Fort Ellis, guardian of the gateway to western Montana and manned by infantry and dragoons. Kelsey was not far east of it, the morning he rode on from Bozeman, when he discerned a rider coming on hard.

Presently he was aware that it was a trooper riding with a courier's steady haste.

The man was a corporal, and, as the gap closed between them, he seemed about to pass on with no more than a nod when suddenly he pulled his mount to a stop.

"Ames, by God!" he yelled. "Sergeant Ames!"

Kelsey had reined about, letting his little string jog on. He stared in bewilderment at the sunburned man with the jaunty campaign hat and dusty blue shirt and pants. The horse wore the old familiar trappings of the Seventh.

Then he said, "By God yourself, Larkin! What're you doing way over here?"

"Riding despatch to Ellis, right now." Corporal Larkin was enjoying Kelsey's surprise as much as the unexpected encounter. Reaching across, they shook hands. "And I could ask you the same question. Last fix I had on you, you were running somebody's ranch across the mountains."

"Made the big break finally," Kelsey said. "I'm going on my own. How long have you been out of Fort Lincoln?"

"Not long—and again too long. When we got marching orders for the Big Horn again, I nearly passed a squealing worm. Had all I wanted up there last year, the same as you did. But you quit when your enlistment run out, and I was fool enough to extend mine. What's it going to be like? Are them Nez Percés the tough turkeys we hear they are?"

"They know how to handle themselves."

"Well, they ain't yet come up against the Seventh."

"Figure they will?"

"Damn my big mouth," said Larkin, "but you're a soldier, yourself. From what I hear, the department's mad at Howard and the way he slogs behind the Indians at a safe distance. Been plenty of newspaper criticism. So they sent an outfit that likes a fight."

"Where's it at?"

Larkin grinned. "That's military information, Sergeant. But you can bet Sturgis ain't frittering away time and men beating the canyons. And he ain't riding into any ambush, the way Perry did at White Bird. Them Indians have got to come down from the mountains sometime. Unless they want to head for Mexico, there's only one way they can come."

"If he thinks he can suck them into an ambush, he's crazy."

"Near as we can tell, they don't even know he's in the country. He's been throwing Crows at 'em to keep 'em interested, and not letting them see any blue shirts. It's two to one they'll run right into it."

Kelsey felt something deeply disturbing within himself. He said, "Mebbe you can fool them, then. For the glory of the Seventh, I suppose I ought to hope so."

"But you don't?"

"I don't. I've seen what it's like to be on the other side. All those people ever asked was to be let alone. I wish they could be."

A crease had built itself between the Corporal's eyes. He said, "Look, Ames—you'll keep what I said under your hat, won't you?"

"You don't have to ask, man."

Nodding, Larkin said, "Well, I better shag. Been good to see you." He offered his hand.

Shaking it, Kelsey said, "Luck."

"And to you."

The horses had moved on along the trail, then begun to drift and graze. Overtaking them, Kelsey started them again. He knew he had put a wide edge of uneasiness in Larkin with his lack of enthusiasm for Sturgis' plans. The Corporal had spoken too freely, thinking it was to an old trooper who would see things his way. The whole hope of ambushing the Nez Percés would be washed away if they were given but an inkling of the fact that a new army was in the field against and ahead of them.

What a long way he had traveled since the days when he had forked a cavalry saddle as a way of life! Then there had been a clear-cut enemy, and a man didn't need to know why that was so. He got orders and took the field with his comrades, and when bullets and arrows started mixing, he fought for his life. No problems, no regrets, and no ambitions but to stay alive. . . .

He came to the Yellowstone at the Benson's Landing ferry crossing, where he halted to noon. Afterward he drifted on, suddenly aimless, without eagerness or pleasure in the thought of hunting up his own range. There was more involved than the fact that he would find it tasteless without his woman to share it.

He knew the present country well enough to realize that, leaving the higher country, the Nez Percés would have to come down into this river valley by way of Rock Creek or Clark's Fork. There was a settlement on the Yellowstone near where they would strike it, a place called Coulson. Now the Nez Percés had become Teal, who was his woman, and so were a part of him whether he would have it so or not.

Night caught him well past the big bend of the river, and on the following evening he rode into Coulson. It was isolated, serving a few scattered ranches and wayfarers. There were a store, a trail station, and two or three weathered houses. He put up at the station for the night, with his horses pegged out along the river.

He knew by morning that he was going to try to get in touch with Teal somehow, and save her from the certain disaster he saw descending upon her trailmates. He could not bring himself to betray Larkin's confidence and, in so doing, his old comrades and his very country. He could not save the others, but Teal would not need to know that he wanted her to come with him for any other reason than that he loved her and had from the day he first saw her at Johnny Hite's fort.

A plan sprang full-blown into his mind, one that was simple but might prove dangerous. The town of Cooke City sat high in the Bear Tooths and was on the route the Nez Percés would need to use coming down from the high plateaus. He would arrange to leave his extra horses here, and a day and a half of hard riding would put him at Cooke. If he had to explain his actions, he would claim to be exploring for suitable range.

He arranged for pasturage for his horses and struck out to the southwest. Around noon he met a platoon of cavalry moving downcountry and to the north, which puzzled him. But they passed him incuriously and were soon swallowed in the rolling terrain. Later a small party of Crow Indians scudded across the horizon and was gone. He followed the river, coming into timber of spruce, fir, and lodgepole pine. There he made a late camp.

He awakened on the gray side of dawn with a sense of uneasiness. He sat up to find himself looking at three men who stared back from beyond pointed rifles. Neither their trail-stained buckskins nor their dark faces told him whether they were Crows or Nez Percés. But he spread his hands outwardly to show their emptiness and tipped his head at them. Then he rose slowly.

"Anybody talk my language?" he asked. When that brought no answer, he reached into his shirt pocket and drew forth his tobacco and cigarette papers. He handed these to the nearest warrior, who took them without any change of facial expression.

The makings passed from hand to hand, and all three warriors managed to shape up something resembling a cigarette. Kelsey struck a match, held it forth while they puffed the smokes alive, then broke the matchstick with a grin.

"Good luck," he said, and no man nodded then, betraying that he understood.

"Nez Percés?" Kelsey asked, trying to sound as if he found nothing alarming about the situation.

A grunt confirmed that surmisal. Then they began talking in their own tongue, and one of the warriors seemed hostile. The one who appeared to understand English said something placating, which had no affect. For a moment it looked dead certain to Kelsey that he was going to be shot. Then the more moderate one pointed to his saddle and the horse that grazed nearby.

"You come," he said.

While wholly blind to the motive behind the order, Kelsey was satisfied. If they were going to kill him, it seemed logical that they would do it here. If he was to be questioned as to his presence in the region or sounded out for military information, he would be taken to the chiefs. He had met Joseph, and through him he could reach Teal. Showing no fear of his captors, he walked out to bring up his horse.

Presently he found himself riding on up the river, as he had already intended, but now with three hostile rifles at his back. He realized by then that they were advance scouts of the Nez Percé band, which itself was much nearer than he had guessed.

From a high bench he saw in the far distance a part of the main Nez Percé village coming slowly on. Some of the people were mounted, but most trudged patiently afoot.

Again his captors talked unintelligibly, then two of them whipped off along the way they had come. Kelsey felt considerable relief at finding himself left with the one halfway amiable man.

He said, "I'd like to see Joseph. I met him through a friend of mine. A girl. I don't know how you say her name, but the white people call her Teal. Teal Shannon."

The warrior shook his head and pointed to the west.

It was a moment before Kelsey understood what was meant, and when he did his spirits sank. This was only a part of the band, then, and Joseph or Teal or both were traveling farther west, which would be along the trail that passed nearer to Cooke City. He all but groaned.

Now there was no estimating what he was up against, and he began to censure himself bitterly. He could discern that the scouts had not wanted him to go free for fear that he would spread the word down-country that the band was coming out of the mountains. Now, even if his life was spared again, there was no telling how long he would be held.

He said, "Look, my friend. I came up here because I want to see this girl and for no other reason. I want to marry her. Her brothers are Running Wolf and Ten Owl, and maybe you know them. They're my friends, too, and I slept in their tepee. I know that afterward some of your people thought I betrayed you at the Big Hole. But I didn't, and she knows I didn't. Can't you take me to her or tell me how to find her?"

The man shook his head. "No good."

"What's going to happen to me?"

"Maybe die." The brave jerked a thumb in the direction his companions had taken. "They know Big Hole. They know you. They say no spy again."

The dots in the distance were growing larger. For a moment despair ran in Kelsey, then decision came. Whatever they believed, he had not wronged these people. He would stand on that record and take his chances.

Without seeming to lift his gaze from Kelsey, his companion began to turn his pony in a slow, short circle. Presently Kelsey saw three horsemen peel off from the group below and ride forward. At a grunt from his guard, Kelsey turned his own horse down the bench. The three Indians rode toward them. They called questions that were identifiable only by their rising inflection. The guard answered them briefly.

The head man in the newly arrived party was identified when, at the end of the talk, the others all looked toward a stocky, youngish fellow who stared at the ground.

A grunt, and the leader turned his horse and started back toward the crawling village, the other two following. Kelsey would have started his horse after them, but his guard shook his head.

"Chief Olicott say we go."

"To the girl?"

"To Joseph."

Kelsey could hardly repress his elation. It would bring him close enough to Teal so that he could see her.

CHAPTER FOURTEEN

THE main body of the Nez Percés moved patiently eastward to the buffalo grounds. The way ran above the timberline, where only scrub timber and bright alpine flowers grew, while the rocky, snow-capped mountains vanished into drifting clouds.

The warrior halted to wait on a rocky point ahead and above the line of march, which was a scout's way of making quick contact with his superiors. Again horsemen turned out from the column to ride a quartering course forward. Kelsey recognized Joseph among the squad that climbed the point. There was a quick glint of recognition in his eyes before his mask of passivity dropped back.

As the Indians talked, Joseph's gaze shifted to Kelsey again and again, probing, weighing. Then the Chief spoke to one of the others, who rode swiftly back toward the band. Those remaining fell silent, watching the progress of the people below.

Soon two figures were riding back. One was slight, and Kelsey felt the beat of his heart speed up. But they were halfway up the slope before he confirmed his strong hope that Joseph had sent for Teal, maybe to interpret or to give an opinion.

There was none of an Indian's repression on Teal's face as she put her pony up the slant ahead of her companion. Her mouth was open, and Kelsey felt a shock at the extent to which the hot sun had bleached her hair and darkened her face and arms.

"Oh, why did you come back?" she said, and that was her only greeting.

"I had to."

Joseph spoke to her then, and Kelsey watched a sudden confusion seep into her face. There was a dry, all but amused quirk to her mouth when she looked back at Kelsey.

"He says you've come to marry me."

"If you're willing."

"I—I don't understand it."

"I've broken with my life the way it was before I met you. I'll have no other unless you'll help me make it."

"Oh, my dear."

For a long moment Teal Shannon looked down upon her people as they moved patiently past. Joseph spoke to his men. They rode away to join the broad, ragged column, but the Chief remained.

Then Teal said, "Do you realize that your life depends on whether I want to marry you?"

"Without you I have no life. Do you want to?"

"Yes. But I can't."

She turned to Joseph and said something that was answered briefly.

"I've told him I love you," she continued in English. "I asked him to entrust you to me. But he wants to ask you some questions first. Do you know if there are any enemies ahead of us besides the Crows?"

Kelsey had dreaded that question, had tried to persuade himself that for the sake of the noncombatants he ought to tell Joseph that a large force of cavalry waited down the country, hoping to pull off a successful ambush. But the taint of disloyalty amounting to treason was on that course.

He said, "Tell him that if I would betray my own people, then he would be justified in fearing that I might betray his."

When Joseph had heard that, he nodded and rode off.

"He's smarter than you think," Teal said. "Because you answered his question through your reluctance."

"I hope he doubles his caution. Teal, you've done all you can for your people. I think your brothers would tell you to come with me."

"They would."

"Then come."

"I can't be good for you. Look what I seem to have done to your life already. I didn't want to, Kelsey—at least, the better part of me didn't. I know what it's like to be caught between two worlds. You'd be, too, because I'd rather give up your world than mine."

He swung from the saddle and held up his arms, but she refused to come down to him. He did not press her because there was something close to awe in him for this girl, for the depths in her, for the dignity and strict discipline of self. A man did not override such things with naked passion.

He said, "But my world isn't the one I left, it's the one I'm hunting. If you won't come with me, let me stay with you. We'll be married the way the Nez Percés do it, and I'll be mighty honored."

"Don't make it sound so easy."

The village had passed them, and its trail dust began to blot it from view. She stared after it, and there was suddenly a kind of elation in her face. He watched it rise, and then he had to watch it be extinguished by the dedication she had imposed upon herself.

He said, "Nothing ought to be as hard as we always make it."

"You go," she said. "My people were greatly discouraged when the Crows turned against us. Now our only hope is to make it to the British Possessions. If we do, come to me there. If we don't, forget me."

"Never. And I won't leave you to your fate till then. If you won't come with me, then I'll stay with you. Forever. That's my decision, Teal. You can't change it."

"They won't let you stay unless I marry you."

"How's it done?"

She almost cried and she almost smiled as she lifted her hands in perplexity. Then resolutely she said, "I won't even talk about it. If we cross the border in safety, then I'll marry you. Not before. That's *my* decision, Kelsey, and let that be the end of it."

He knew that he had lost. She had set herself a course from which she would not turn, out of despair or out of a newer longing. He weighed the right and wrong of letting her cling to her hope of escape, of eventual freedom for her people, when he might have told her how great was the force massed against them. But that would be to destroy the very thing he loved in her most. It would be to win her by making her into something other than what she was.

He said, "Then I'll go."

She swung down and came into his arms. Her kiss was free and fiercely longing, but the barrier between them was almost a taste upon her lips. Her face had sagged a little by the time they stepped apart, and in that moment he might have overwhelmed her. But he did not.

He said, "I'll be with you every step of the way. If you make it, I'll be there soon. If you don't, then you or God Himself can't keep me from sharing whatever you have to undergo."

He saw her go up on her horse and swing away, and he watched until the timber had blotted her out. Then he hit leather again himself and headed on down the trail. A mile and then a thousand miles were between them again. But it was different now. He had seen Teal, and they were promised, even if that promise could not be fulfilled this side of kingdom come . . .

He returned to Coulson on the Yellowstone with no idea of what he would do with himself during what might be a long and dreadful wait for Teal. But he had barely ridden into the little settlement when he discerned a familiar figure on the road station porch. The man rose up instantly, disclosing that he had been waiting and watching the river trail.

The very improbability of his presence here at this remote place stunned Kelsey. He gasped, "Halverson! What in hell are you doing over here?"

"Waiting for you, friend."

"You been trailing me?"

"It wasn't hard to do." There was little of the belligerence in the man that Kelsey would have expected. Instead, Lafe Halverson's plump, pink face wore a half-smile that on the surface seemed benign. "Trace asked me to do it. He wants you set straight on things for his girl's sake. That's the only reason I'd bother."

"Where do you figure to set me straight, man?"

"I learned you left your horses here. Come to get them? Then let's take a little walk down where they are."

"You can say your say here, Halverson."

"Come on. I don't want any eavesdropping."

Shrugging, Kelsey swung down. Leading his horse, he walked beside the man for whom he bore a killing hatred, partly out of curiosity as to what Trace wanted said. When they were out of earshot of the settlement's huddled buildings, he halted.

"Well?"

"Look," Halverson said mildly. "You made some mighty serious charges to Trace about me. Had him believing them, almost, which fact Riskin used to his own advantage. I'd like to know what you base all that on."

"In Lewiston," Kelsey retorted, "I come in on you and Ben talking mighty hush-hush. Before you broke off, you told him to leave things up to Chappy. A while back I killed Ben and Billy and stopped them from running whisky to the Crows. That was bad enough. But three of Trace's teamsters were murdered in getting that booze. In Idaho a couple more people were murdered to incite feeling against the Nez Percés."

"Those are the facts," Halverson said readily. "But you see them dead wrong. I knew the Riskin boys were no good. You heard me trying to stop Ben from running with them. I sort of liked the man. Then you got Trace scared of me. Riskin caught on and threatened to suck us both in with him, knowing you'd back him in it. But I got Trace straightened out. He wanted me to do the same for you."

"Why?"

"He wants you to come home."

"Tell him he can go sing."

"All right," Halverson said, still unruffled. "Then there's another chore. I want to make contact with Joseph and don't know a soul I'd trust who could do it. From what I hear about you, I reckon you could. In fact, I expect that's where you've just been."

"What do you want of Joseph?"

"I'm putting a big cache of food and medical supplies in the Big Snowies. I want him to be looking for it when he passes through."

"You're *what?*"

Grinning, Halverson said, "I reckon you heard. You'd never believe it of me, would you? But I want to help him get through to Sitting Bull. So do you. What does it matter if our reasons aren't the same? We both want that, and we can work together to get it."

"Didn't think you'd shown your real hand," Kelsey said. "And I reckon I know what you're up to. If Joseph knows there'll be caches along the way for him, he'll try all the harder to make the border. If he gets across, there'll be a threat of trouble from him and Sitting Bull for a long while. That means manned forts throughout the country, and you've got your precious contracts. Halverson, you can stick on an idea like some can on a bronc."

"Don't you want them to escape?"

"Reckon so."

"All right. Tell Joseph what I said. It will take him to the British Possessions. And Sitting Bull will receive him if he thinks he can get a good backer that way himself."

"You'd back what are enemies of your country?"

"No harm in letting them think I would. And you're about ready to throw in with those so-called enemies yourself, aren't you, Ames?"

"I'm trying to help the girl I love and otherwise not to take sides at all." Kelsey made a flat, dismissing motion with his hand. "As far as helping you is concerned, I'd rather drill you."

At last the amiability began to drain out of Halverson's face. He studied Kelsey through narrowed lids for a moment. "About this girl you are currently in love with," he said in an almost toneless voice. "I understand Chappy swore revenge against you through somebody you care about."

"Now it comes—the real business."

"Maybe. Suppose Chappy learns you've transferred your affections, Ames?"

Bitterly Kelsey said, "Trace tell you about it to protect his daughter? Or did Glenna do it out of revenge?"

"Does it matter? There'll be supplies cached all along the way for the Nez Percés. There'll be more backing after he gets across. You remember that. It could be you'll reach the conclusion that you'd better play ball."

"I reckon we've had our little talk out," Kelsey said. "You'll work against them or for them, as best suits your own purpose. We may have the same hopes about their reaching the border safe and sound. But what I do to help, I'll do on my own."

"Don't give yourself cause for regrets."

"Don't you give me more cause to kill you than I already have."

It was Halverson who broke it off, heeling about and walking back up to the trail.

Kelsey would have given much to know if Trace had helped plot this new move, made necessary from Halverson's viewpoint that the Nez Percés obviously were not going to receive help enough to fight a major war south of the border. It was easy to understand why they would pick him to act as a go-between with Joseph. A man who could be threatened was also a man who could be trusted to keep his mouth shut.

By the time he had rounded up his horses and got them ready to train, Halverson had disappeared. Kelsey paid for the grazing, swung aboard his saddler, and rode out, heading north up Canyon Creek. He had a strong hunch that if there was to be more contraband running, Riskin was the man Halverson would use to do it. So, ahead in the Big Snowy Mountains, there might be a chance to make contact with Chappy. That was the only way to guarantee that Teal would not suffer the experience of the Golden girl, so far back now on the trail.

CHAPTER FIFTEEN

H E was now upon the prairie, the great rolling sea of buffalo grass, dry coulees, and rugged buttes that ran past the horizon and past the border to the British domain. Except for cottonwood and alder along the streams, there were no trees. And except for white-tailed jack rabbits, chattering prairie dogs, and an occasional rattlesnake, there seemed to be no life.

He pitched camp in Canyon Creek. The Nez Percés must come this way, there being only one place in a reach of a hundred miles where the Missouri could be crossed. That was the great danger to them, the predictability of their route once they had set themselves upon a direct course for the border. It would be either a race or a fight to the Cow Island crossing; beyond there it would be a short and simple jump to sanctuary.

The next day he pressed on, coming down into the valley of the Musselshell for his camp, finding a shallow winding stream that emptied into the Missouri. The days were growing cool now, the nights cold, reminding him of how narrowly the Nez Percés were crowding the savagery of a prairie winter.

On the day following, there rose in the far forward distance the hazy uplift of low mountains. Excitement quickened in him as he traveled steadily. Up there, along a line marked by this old trapper route, lay the place where Halverson had promised to make a cache for Joseph. That same place might well be his own rendezvous, Kelsey believed, with Chappy Riskin.

He figured that he had several days to kill, and as the country began to interest him more and more, he knew what he would do to while away the time. He camped near the summit to spend an uncomfortably chilly night. The next morning he made a very careful inspection of the vicinity, then broke camp and rode out down the western slope toward the Carroll trail and the gap that broke in upon the wheeling basin of the Judith. He was convinced that he would make his contact here or not at all.

The great, fertile valley was still buffalo country, prized and contested among the Indians for vast distances about. But where buffalo ran, cattle and horses could prosper. The encircling mountains gave to the valley a plentiful rainfall. This was it, the place where he would stake out his wild range—his and Teal's. Here he would remove the threat to her imposed by Riskin, and here he would wait for her and her people to come along.

By night he had found the place, between the Judith headwaters and a northward flowing fork. He pitched his camp where he would build a cabin of cottonwood from the river timber. He turned his horses loose on what would be their home range and, rolled up in his blanket, he long watched the stars he would forever see with his wife. He was for the first time in his life completely satisfied.

He had much to do before winter. Teal would live in a tepee if necessary, but he would have to bring in supplies. He would need corrals and something resembling a barn for his stock. In the spring he would begin to trap mustangs, and he would buy and bring in a good blooded stallion to cross with them. He did not care how long it took, but he was going to set himself up in the business of raising horses for the market.

He rose the next morning in a crisp dawn. He cooked a quick breakfast, brought in his horse, and saddled up. Two hours' riding put him on the trail, which he cut back and forth for a considerable distance without seeing any sign of recent travel. But he had set himself a task of great patience, and because he dared not miss his chance, he mounted a rim where he could quietly watch the trail that ran out of the purpled southern obscurity.

Glenna seemed much farther behind him than the days that had elapsed since he left Butte. Stolidly waiting and watching, he could not help projecting her against this primitive region. If he had never before recognized her unfitness for his way of life, he did now. She would see in this only an ugly solitude, while to him it was as close to heaven on earth as a man could get. Even though she might have been party to Trace's invitation to return, Kelsey had no regrets. She was disqualified even without the possibility that she had helped send Chappy Riskin against Teal.

He put in a tedious day, eating cold food from his saddlebags and drinking tepid water from his canteen. At sundown he returned to his camp to cook himself a hot meal and to check on his horses. Then he moved the camp to his vantage point. If the renegade Riskin was doing the job for Halverson, he might prefer to travel at night.

But three days and nights wore past without his having seen anything but the wildlings of the vicinity and, once, a herd of buffalo moving in the far distance. He began to grow restless, at last beginning to question his reasoning, but he knew that he had to see the thing through.

When at last he saw someone of his own kind, it was an Army courier who came whipping along the prairie floor, undoubtedly on his way to Fort Benton. At first

Kelsey was of a mind to keep hidden and let him pass by. But curiosity welled in him. He rode out to intercept the dragoon.

The man reined up in astonishment, yelling, "What in hell are you doing out here, man?" He wore the insignia of the Seventh Cavalry, although Kelsey had never seen him before.

"Hunting me a piece of range."

"You picked a damned poor place to roost. There's a band of wild Injuns headed this way and coming fast."

"Nez Percés?" Kelsey asked.

"Who else?"

"Hell, I thought you people had stopped 'em a long time ago."

"Then you better think again. They sure must have powerful medicine. Sturgis, he hit 'em on Canyon Creek with four hundred men and in complete surprise. But they beat him off and got away in the night. What you grinning for, man? You damned settlers gripe the hell out of me. Always figure you could do it better."

"You still running from 'em?" Kelsey asked, still unable to keep the corners of his mouth from stretching upward.

"Hell with you," the trooper said, and he rode on.

Kelsey knew more than had been told him, and he had learned it without asking questions. The Nez Percés had got around Sturgis successfully, and that was the best news he had heard in a long time. But it was only a reprieve for Joseph and his people, for soon there would be fresh forces in ahead of them again.

The uplift of spirits began to quit him. There still had been a fight on Canyon Creek, and he could not help wondering how Teal had made out. Certainly it would not have put her in a more receptive frame of mind about leaving her people and remaining with him on the Judith ranch. He had hoped that, when she had seen the place, she would reconsider.

Early the next morning his carefully set senses jarred him awake. He had only to place his ear to the ground to detect the distant footfalls of several horses. He knew at once that the time had come and was on his feet in the same moment. He checked his pistol, then quietly went to his picketed horse and saddled it. He had plenty of time. Whoever Halverson was using, the man would make his cache where the Indians would have little trouble finding it. First Kelsey meant to make sure who it was. After that he could plan the rest.

He cut a wide loop, staying above the trail until he had entered the scrub timber on the lower slope of the mountain. Then he pressed in to a place where the coming pack train would cross an open meadow. There was enough starlight so that he thought he might be able to tell something about its handler.

Standing before his horse, his palm on its nostrils to keep it from nickering, he waited in deep shadow. The earth drum grew louder, and then he saw the bell pony of the string break out into the meadow and come on, a dozen other horses following. Kelsey nibbled his lip, not breathing easily until he saw that only one packer rode in the rear, a slumped figure that looked tired in the saddle. He was not certain, but believed that he could discern the sloping shoulders of Riskin.

He let the string toil past, intending to make his play at the place the man chose to drop pack. Rising again to leather, he skirted the route, letting the pack train stay a little ahead of him. His blood and his nerves were on fire.

The packer climbed on for a couple of miles into the highlands and then brought the string to a stop. Swinging down, Kelsey secured his horse in a clump of scrub pine, then prowled forward on foot, his gun in his hand. The packer had dismounted, his animals grouping tiredly. The man started forward on foot, and Kelsey yelled at him.

"Riskin, haul about! This time we settle it."

He was only then exactly sure of his man. The high-shouldered body swung, and it was clearly Chappy Riskin who made a stabbing reach at his pistol. This time there was no shelter into which he could plunge, and this time a nursed hatred added its weight. He cursed softly, drew, and fired from where he stood.

Kelsey did not crowd his advantage, having no mind to hedge his own security in this thing he had to do. He shot when he knew the odds were balanced, wove to the right, and fired again. But Riskin set off no second shot. The shoulders jerked higher, and the gun dropped from a suddenly spread hand. He crumpled slowly to the ground.

Running forward, Kelsey swept up the dropped pistol. But Riskin did not stir, and there was no breath or pulse in him when Kelsey bent over him. For an instant Kelsey shut his eyes, the shock of violence sickening him. But there was no regret. Had this been done a year ago, he knew of at least seven people who would now be living. A year from now there would be people alive who might not be with Riskin still in business.

Only when Kelsey had thrown off the tensions of his long vigil and final fight did he begin to realize the responsibilities he had taken upon himself. Examining the packs, he found that they contained exactly what Halverson had promised to furnish the Indians—food, medicine, and bandage materials, items that were desperately needed.

He had to decide whether he was going to turn them over to the Nez Percés, if and when they came past. He wanted to do that more than he had ever wanted anything in his life. His purpose in pursuing and finishing Riskin had not had much bearing on the man's business here, but upon the threat he had made and would have tried to carry out.

Yet he had to square this death with the authorities, and in so doing he needed reasons greater than personal enmity and a more accurate marksmanship. Therefore he had to take the pack train and its contraband over to Fort Benton, together with the body. That would use up all of three days' time, going and coming, if he was allowed to return. It would be another act against Teal, even as it had been one for her, and he wondered if she would understand why he did it.

He had returned to pick up his own horses when something caused him to pause, hand on the horn, to listen closely before mounting. He swung up to the saddle with a puzzled frown, aware that other horses were coming on along the backtrail. Worry turned in him, for he had not supposed that there would be two sections of the pack train. He rode deeper into the timber, then came out afoot where he could watch the oncomers ride into the meadow where Riskin's loaded animals were now scattered and grazing.

It was not another pack string, but three riders, and they halted at once when they saw the horses. For a moment they seemed to talk together, then they rode on cautiously. He saw them pull down again at the place where Riskin lay. Their excited movements failed to reveal whether they were friends of the man or stray travelers. Kelsey rode out toward them, calling out to reassure them.

"Howdy, friends!"

The three men had dismounted, and they whipped about. But since his gun was holstered and his approach open, they showed no immediate hostility.

"You kill this shytepoke?" a man called back.

"I reckon so."

Kelsey felt easier as he closed the gap. One of the men was dressed in town clothes, while the other two wore the garb of the range.

"Name's Ames," he said, "and I'm right glad you come along. This man was a renegade and more. He was a killer running from the law."

"We never just happened along," said the man in the store clothes. "I'm Frank Judkins, and I run a store in Radersburg. Two days ago a man come in and arranged for me to send supplies to Colonel Sturgis on the Musselshell. My packer barely got into the Big Belts when he was jumped. Shot and wounded, but he got away. When he got back to town, me and the boys here set out to catch that pack train. This is it."

"And is this the man who ordered the stuff?" Kelsey said, pointing at the still figure on the ground.

"Not him. The man was—"

"Wait," Kelsey cut in. "Convince you better if I done the describing. He was short and stocky, with red cheeks."

"That's the fellow."

"Well, there's your pack train, and you can take the body in with you. His name was Riskin. Any sheriff will recognize it. And the man who tried to fool you answers to the name of Lafe Halverson. Comes from Lewiston. I'll leave that up to you, but if I'm wanted, I'm staking a claim on the upper Judith. I was watching for Riskin. I had a tip he'd try to run contraband to the Nez Percés. Not out of the goodness of his heart. He wants a real war, any way he can get one, the same as Lafe Halverson."

"You the Ames who used to work for Trace Buckmaster?"

"That's right."

"Heard about you stopping a run of whisky to the Crows. So I reckon you're in the clear, and I'm obliged. It wasn't only the supplies and horses and the man they might have killed. It sure graveled me to be taken in that way. Maybe I'm a fool, but I hate to have it showed up so plain."

Since it was wild country and there was danger from stray Crows or Sioux as well as the oncoming Nez Percés, Judkins and his trailmates ate and rested only briefly before starting back. The last thing Kelsey did was to place an order of his own with Judkins and arrange for it to be packed to his new camp on the Judith. Then he headed back to that camp.

There was a sense of fulfillment in the successful conclusion of his long, grim vigil. But a new wait must begin at once, for he meant to get in touch with Teal again when her people came through the vicinity. He could not give up his hope of yet being able to take her out of that long and grueling march.

But it was two more days before, waiting in the Judith gap, he discerned raised dust in the far southern distance. It was mass movement, and he watched two hours to be sure it was not buffalo. The progress was steadily his way, and when at last he could discern both mounted and walking people, he devised a plan for making contact that would be less dangerous and cumbersome than the ones he had used before.

He kept hidden and let the Indians on advance guard ride through, reflecting as he had before that Joseph's main error on the march was his failure to scout far enough ahead. Then, as the big contingent came into plainer view, Kelsey mounted his horse and rode out onto the bench ahead of them. He rode the horse in the slow circle he had seen the Indians use. He knew that to the Indians' sharp eyes his garb would reveal him as a white man.

He grinned when, only minutes later, he saw two

mounted ponies cut ahead, riding toward him. His eyes glued on the small shape he believed to be Teal's.

It was Teal and her brother Ten Owl. She bent on her horse and whipped it forward, leaving the man to trail her. Her mouth was open as she rode up the slope.

"Howdy," he said. "I figured that maybe you'd like a holiday. So I aim to show you our ranch and let you pick out the place for the cabin."

He swung down as she slid from her pony's bare back, and he didn't care if the whole Nez Percés nation watched him sweep her into his arms. She said nothing at first, only sobbing in her surprise and happiness. When they stepped apart, she fiercely held onto his hands.

"I'm so glad to see you all in one piece!" she breathed.

"I was plenty exercised myself," he said, "after I heard about the Canyon Creek fight. Did you make out all right?"

"They didn't get close to the women that time. Darling, you hadn't ought to be way off here by yourself!"

Considering her own situation, he had to laugh at her worrying about him. He said, "I'm going to make one more bid for you to change your mind. Let's get married and spend a day or two at my camp. Then, if you still want to, we can catch up with the march and go with it to the border. Won't you?"

"Oh, Kelsey, I—I don't know." Her words ran out on a sigh, and their clear uncertainty gave him a spurt of hope.

Ten Owl had halted at a distance below. Kelsey

beckoned to him, and he came on. Teal said something that brought a smile to the face of the brother.

"Tell him you would?" Kelsey asked anxiously.

"Yes, darling. I told him I would."

"When?"

"At tonight's camp."

CHAPTER SIXTEEN

So it was done, the wedding feast, the gifts, the acceptance of his bride. The feast was of horse flesh and a little corn brought from the far-off Clearwater. His gift was that of his watch to Running Wolf, and his bride was the slim, brown-skinned girl with the shining eyes.

It shocked him to see the fare on which the Indians were living, their rags, their sickness and sores and unhealed wounds. In spite of his happiness, guilt rose in him at the memory of the pack train he had returned to Radersburg. Whether or not good could come of evil, that would have helped.

Then, as the tired camp quieted down from the brief festivities, he and Teal rode out together. They picked up his temporary camp and pressed on at once for the claim, where he wanted it to be—their first night together.

A thousand stars flung their light upon them, and a score of wildlings added sound to the swift footfalls of the horses. Yet the riders were content with silence, in respite from care, and in what he knew had been her deciding hope—that the border, now so near, would be reached without further disaster.

When at last they had come to the place he had picked for them, he swept an arm about to include the whole starlit vicinity.

"This is it—all ours."

"Oh, wonderful!"

"The cabin will be here by the river, where there's timber and shade. The range will run as far as the eye can see, and God help the man who tries to take it from me. Tough at first, though. Maybe nothing better than a tepee this winter."

"Who cares?"

They made a quick camp. Afterward, she said, "Sometimes I've thought I'd go to jail for life if they'd promise me a bath in return. But I've no clean clothes. Can you help me out?"

"Shirt and pants."

"Soap?"

"Plenty."

"Now I know why I married you. For your wealth."

Presently she slipped off to the river, while he sat smoking and tasting the richness of the deep solitude. He was not worried when she did not return for some time, but presently he threw away his cigarette and moved quietly down toward the water.

She was toweling, and his breath caught as he looked upon the slim loveliness of her body. Then, as if feeling the weight of his attention, she turned her head. She made a small outcry and hastily pulled the towel to her. Then he heard the sound of her laugh, and the towel fell as he went on toward her. . . .

He awakened to see dark clouds drifting across the sky. Teal was still soundly asleep, a soft, curled shape beside him. He lay for a long moment just watching the faint flare of her nostrils as her breath came and went. It was as if he had never known another woman, for in her he had found depths of feeling, depths of caring he had not known could be.

But the sky hinted too loudly of winter for him to be lazy long. He rose and started a breakfast fire, then went to the river for fresh water. She was still asleep when he came back, so he started to make breakfast, knowing it would be the first good meal she had eaten in weeks. An infinite sympathy and tenderness rose in him. He had done his best to play the game straight, not only with her Indian brethren but with their mutual white fellowship. Yet he was ready to admit at last that when it came to this pitiful, desperate dash for freedom, he was all on the side of the Nez Percés. He could for the first time plainly see what had held her so stubbornly to her chosen course of action.

He had not wanted to shatter her hopes of ultimate escape, and would not now. But he was worried, remembering the courier who had gone to Fort Benton for Colonel Sturgis, remembering the other Army cantonments and forts within striking reach of this place.

He was not aware that Teal had awakened until he heard her say, "Lordy, it's going to rain!"

"Got to sometime. Roll out of there, Smoky, and come get your breakfast."

He watched the smooth skin of her back as, turned away from him, she sat up in the blankets and struggled into the clothes he had lent her. He grinned as she stood up in them, all but lost.

"Like it?" she asked uncertainly.

"Long as I can find the girl in there."

"Wouldn't take her long to get out."

It both amused and touched him to see her try to hold back her long hunger. So he wolfed his own food, paying her no outward notice, and her plate was clean as quickly as was his own. He filled it again, but she shook her head, saying, "Better not. I'm not used to it."

"You'll never be hungry again. I got a man coming with supplies from Radersburg. Enough to winter us. Besides, there's more game than we'll ever eat around here. River's full of fish. Where do you want the cabin?"

She cast judicious eyes about and said, "Let's take a look at the whole shebang."

They spent most of the day exploring their domain. It was government land, not even open officially to white settlement. But nobody ever bothered the intrepid ones who dared to enter such regions, and later, Kelsey knew, their claim would be respected not only by the authorities, but also by the other settlers who were bound to follow them.

The rain held off until late afternoon, and then it made them run for camp. He had prepared for it by using a tarpaulin to make a lean-to against the trunk of a big tree. Laughing, Teal ran into it and threw herself flat on the blankets. He kindled a fire in front, then moved in with her, removing his dripping hat. He heard her sigh of contentment, and when he glanced down she was watching him ever so closely, with all her love standing in her eyes.

He leaned down, and as their mouths came together the fire seemed to sweep all about them. In the rain's sibilance upon the leaves, they were again united, and afterward they lay together in silent dreaming. For the briefest moment he thought of the sumptuous ranch house he had left for this, and was wholly without regrets.

The rain continued the next morning, cold and dismal, and he sensed a restlessness in Teal. He knew that the respite she had allowed herself was over, that she could not wholly relax until she could put worry out of her mind permanently. It was he that suggested they break camp.

"How long to the border from here?" she asked.

"They're two days march ahead and should be close to the Cow Island crossing. Three days humping, after that, would put them across the line."

"You say 'would.' Why don't you say 'will'?"

"Will, then. If they can cross the Missouri, I don't see much that could stand against 'em. There's still troops at Fort Benton, Teal, and we can't be sure they won't put in their bid. By the time we catch up, we'll know."

"You really want to come?"

"You couldn't keep me from it."

"I won't even try. I couldn't be away from you now. I'm a hussy, but I've dreamed of being with you ever since I met you."

"Should have married me in the mountains."

"I was sorry afterward. But don't you see? I was so bitter about what happened in Idaho that I swore to stay with my people forever, to experience what they did, to accept nothing better. Know who helped me change my mind, when it came to my man?"

"Your brothers, I expect."

She shook her head. "Chief Joseph. He's one of the wisest men I know. When he learned I'd sent you away, up there, he said, 'How is it you can help us by refusing the man you love?' I don't think anyone can think straighter than an Indian, and I realized I was only punishing you for other people's sins."

They broke camp, taking along the pack outfit but leaving his string of horses. Striking north through the basin, they soon cut the broad trail of the Nez Percés. Held back by the foot marchers, the Indians could cover no more distance in the time elapsed than good saddle horses could cross in a day.

The rain continued, and the air grew colder. It was unfamiliar country to Kelsey, but in late afternoon he thought he could see the Missouri breaks, far ahead of them.

The last highland finally gave them a view of the river. Beyond rose the long, low lifts of the Little Rockies, while on the near side the refugee caravan had come to a spread-out halt.

Teal said, "There they are! But aren't those people across the river, too? It looks like a big camp."

"Sure does," Kelsey agreed, squinting against the misty distance. He felt a riffle of uneasiness. Without field glasses, he could not determine what it was that dotted the shore on the north side under the yellow river bluff. "Looks like a pile of stores a steamboat must have left on the bank. That's a guard detachment."

"Not military!"

"Dunno what else it could be, honey." He looked at her thoughtfully. She was wearing his poncho now, as well as the other clothes he had lent her, and there was nothing to tag her as being even partly Indian. "I got an idea we better keep back a while. Nobody would guess you belong to that village. We might pick up some information."

"There aren't so very many of them over there," she said, but she did not sound relieved.

They sat their horses, watching the movement below at the river's edge. Kelsey realized that the chiefs themselves had been given pause by what they had come upon at this, the only crossing in many miles. A file of some twenty warriors entered the water and began to splash boldly across the wide, tawny stream. Their progress was not challenged. The rest of the people followed, then the pack train and pony herd crossed, and there still was no dispute.

Kelsey was dead sure that it was an Army dump there on the north side, and that it had been left under guard. He knew that at this season Cow Island was the head of navigation for the steamboats coming up the Missouri from far-off river forts and towns. The supplies could be intended for Fort Benton, or they could mean something of a more sobering significance. This could be an advance dump laid down for a force coming up the river from some more easterly post.

As if reading his dark thoughts, Teal said, "Something's bad. What is it?"

"Well, I'm sure that's two-three squads of soldiers over there. Too few to put up much of a fight. But they'll have to fight or run. When Joseph sees that's Army chuck and maybe ammunition, he's going to help himself. God knows he's needed a chance like this for a long, long time."

"If the soldiers don't fight, they won't be hurt," Teal said. "That's been the rule from the start. But we do need supplies. There hasn't been a chance to hunt since we reached buffalo country."

As the Nez Percés emerged on the far side, they began to poke about the supply dump and were not molested by the guard. Kelsey could see none of the latter now, and hoped they had possessed the good sense to take to the hills. Apparently that was the case, for soon Indians were swarming all over the stores, hunting and helping themselves.

Presently some of them began to head on toward a creek that came down through the bluffs, the way the pack train and pony herd had already gone. The head men seemed to be hurrying the laggards, and it was not long before they had all thinned out from the river flats.

Then a rifle cracked somewhere, and Teal let out a cry.

Dusk was coming in swiftly. Kelsey felt his jaw muscles tighten as other rifles took up the refrain. But it soon petered out, then presently he saw flames begin to lick at the supply heap. The last of the Nez Percé warriors had set what was left on fire and were going on. He let out a sigh of relief.

"Now what?" Teal asked.

"We're going down and inquire if we can camp there tonight for safety," Kelsey told her. "Our story will be true as far as it goes. We've taken land in the Judith basin. They'll suppose that the Nez Percés scared us into hunting company, and we won't disillusion 'em."

"You're ready to spy on your own people?"

"Look here," he said roughly. "Quit saying my people and yours. You've got white blood in you. My kids'll have Indian blood in them. I'm not going to spy, but if there's been an army trying to beat Joseph to this crossing, which seems likely, then I'd like to know it."

"You'd tell Joseph?"

"I'd sure tell him to get the lead out of his pants."

When he came out of the ford with Teal, the burning dump was a great torch in the twilight. The military guard, he saw, had thrown up a breastwork at a distance, more intent upon protecting themselves than the stores. He noted around a dozen blue-shirted infantrymen, with three or four civilians, who all watched puzzledly as the newcomers topped the bank and rode in on them. A man with a sergeant's stripes came forward.

"You people are flirting with trouble," he said quietly.

"And plenty willing to quit," Kelsey answered. "We

watched the little ruckus from the ridge back yonder. I'm Ames, recently of Butte and before that of the Seventh Cavalry. This is my wife."

The sergeant touched his hat to Teal, saying, "Honored, ma'am. I'm Sergeant Moelchert of the Seventh Infantry. Same number as your husband's, except us poor sons have to walk. But what are you doing out here?"

"Just put hanks on a piece of land in the Judith," Kelsey answered. "Looks like there's been a steamboat here lately."

"The Benton. She just went back."

"Time like this, a man wouldn't mind being on her."

"You're not the only ones," Moelchert said, grinning. "But I reckon you'd be safe if you went back to your claim. Miles is on the Musselshell with part of your old outfit. And I sent a runner to Benton. They never got here in time to keep the Indians from crossing river. But they'll sure keep 'em from crossing back."

Nodding at the burning supply dump, Teal said, "What did the Indians take?"

"Only what little they could carry. Mostly beans and flour and hardtack."

"Well," Kelsey said, "I hope you don't mind us camping kind of close to you tonight."

"Help yourself."

Kelsey took Teal and the pack outfit on downstream until the light of the fire had been swallowed by distance.

"What do you think?" Teal said at last.

"Sounds like there's still plenty of army around," Kelsey reflected. "But with the start Joseph's got, he ought to make it across the line if he watches his back-trail and keeps humping."

"They want to hunt," Teal said. "But they've got a little extra food now. I expect they'll keep going."

"We'll pull out before daylight and catch up."

CHAPTER SEVENTEEN

WHEN Kelsey rode in with his bride, late the next afternoon, he found a relaxed camp on Cow Creek, north of the Little Rockies. Leaden sky stretched over it, vast and empty prairie again ran all about. But there was food captured from the Army, and there were only a few short marches between that place and the dreamed-of border.

The camp was only an overnight halt, and no lodges had been erected. Running Wolf and Ten Owl had their fire on the edge of the creek, among the rank riparian trees that were the only greenery in all that country. When Kelsey had joined them with Teal, she at once took over the cooking of supper, as was an Indian woman's duty, and he seated himself on the sandy earth with a rock against his back and felt his very soul expand again.

He had wondered many times of late why white men believed they were bringing civilization to the country and why they supposed their culture to be superior to that which they would extinguish. More and more he was beginning to realize that right and wrong had little to do with the question, that it was a raw and ugly matter of a greater against a lesser strength, with gain the sole and dreary motive.

He felt an urge to ask Teal to arrange a meeting for him with Joseph, for he had begun to feel less reluctant about warning the chief that Miles was at the mouth of the Musselshell in strength and that Fort Benton had been informed of the Nez Percés' crossing of the Missouri. Now it seemed to him less a matter of frustrating the plans of the Military than of giving these people a decent chance at survival and the escape of cruel and wanton slaughter.

But before he had reached a decision a warrior came to their camp and spoke briefly to Teal. Turning to Kelsey, she said, "There's a white man here to see Joseph. They want me to interpret. Maybe you'd better come."

"White man?" Kelsey was on the point of declining when suddenly he had a deep, intuitive sense that it might be well for him to go along. He could think of only one white man who might want to talk with Joseph bad enough to come all this way and risk the dangers of entering the hostile camp. "Maybe it would be a good idea," he said.

They went down through the cluttered cook fires along the reach of the creek. Joseph and his family had their camp where a cut bank gave a degree of privacy. Coming near, Kelsey saw the Chief seated on the ground. Then his gaze fixed in intensity upon a familiar, stocky figure.

Lafe Halverson looked up and his mouth sagged open.

"Reckon I'll have a few words with the man first, Teal," Kelsey said, and she nodded.

Recovering quickly from the shock of recognition, Halverson made a dry smile.

"Thought you'd be locked up by now, Halverson," Kelsey said.

"The only man who might have got me locked up," Halverson said easily, "is dead. You killed him, I hear. Your guesswork isn't enough for the law to act on, Ames. When will you learn that?"

"You ordered the stuff Riskin took away from the Radersburg packer."

"A proper business. I had an Army order. How could I know what would happen to it?"

"And now?"

"And now to attend to the business you were mule-headed enough to refuse. If the lady is ready to talk to Joseph for me."

"I m ready," Teal said quietly.

There was a glint of wicked relish in Halverson's eyes when he said, "First, tell the Chief that he has taken a man into his camp who is working against him. A man who broke up an effort to gain you help from the Crows. A man who intercepted supplies I tried to get you and sent them back where they came from. Your admirer, ma'am, in case he forgot to tell you."

Kelsey watched Teal's eyes widen in surprise and for the first time regretted his reluctance to inform her about those things. She switched her gaze to him, and she did not speak.

"Afraid to tell Joseph that?" Halverson said, laughing softly.

"I'll hear my husband's side of it first," Teal answered.

"Your husband?" Halverson's eyes widened. "Congratulations."

"It was renegade whisky," Kelsey cut in, "for which three freighters were murdered and scalped to make it look like the work of the Nez Percés. There's a better than even chance it would have worked against you if it had got through to the Crow reservation, seeing how they truckled to the Army. The same man brought the supplies to the Snowies. I had to kill him because this man had threatened you through him. I had to return the stuff because the man it belonged to come along. Even without me, he'd have kept them from being turned over to the Indians. Go ahead and tell Joseph. I trust him."

Teal spoke to the Chief, whose probing gaze shuttled from Kelsey to Halverson. Joseph answered briefly. Then she looked at the visitor with a glint of triumph in her eyes.

"He wants to know what manner of help you offer now."

"Tell him that if he can reach Sitting Bull and form an alliance with him, I'll see that they are equipped to recover their lost lands."

"Chief Joseph says he does not remember that your voice was raised when he needed friends back home. So why do you make this offer?"

"Because his brave and brilliant fight has won my

complete support."

"He won't believe that. Because you are also supplying the Army. Playing one side against the other and in nobody's interest but your own."

"I never come here to talk to you, lady," Halverson snapped. "And I'll thank you to tell him what I said."

Again Teal talked with the Indian leader.

"He says you can perhaps talk to Sitting Bull yourself about it," she reported.

"What does he mean by that?"

"He's not going to let you go until we've crossed the border."

"Now, look here!" Halverson said, standing up quickly. "I come here as a friend, and I'm not going to be monkeyed with!"

"Too bad," Kelsey said. "But that's what happened to me the first time I paid a visit. I had to prove I was reliable, and that's all you got to do. Can you, Halverson?"

"I'll be damned if—" Halverson blustered, then the sand ran out of him, and he slowly shook his head back and forth.

"That's better," Teal said pleasantly. "It will only be for a few days, if you behave yourself. Otherwise you will probably be shot. The Chief quoted a man he and I like very much. He says that if you will betray your own people, then he must assume that you will betray him."

It gave Kelsey a small shock to realize that he had made that much impression upon the Indian leader. It also gave him a sense of vindication in the hard course he had steered for himself.

The chief gave a short, gruff call that brought two warriors on the double. Another order, and they left with Halverson, who for a moment showed a reckless defiance that abruptly died. When they had vanished in the creek brush, Kelsey looked back at Joseph.

He said, "Teal, say to him that I have now reached the place where both sides are my people. I want him to know about the two Army outfits fogging it to catch him before he slips across the border. To my mind he ought to make it a forced march from here on, not stopping for anything."

"Thank you, darling. I might have told him, but I wanted you to. Somehow I thought you would."

"Tell him."

"He already knows. Halverson told him, trying to ingratiate himself. But he'll appreciate your confirmation."

Again Teal and her people's leader talked earnestly.

"He thanks you," Teal interpreted. "But whoever comes after us must cross the river where we did, and he's scouting the backtrail very carefully."

As they returned to their own camp, she caught his hand and held it, and he was very sure of his place with all of them. In that was a pride that six months ago would have surpassed his understanding. It was harder to win an Indian's respect than a white man's, which was strange indeed when these were assumed to be such low-bred people. . . .

Shortly after noon the next day, the marching people came upon a bull train slowly tooling to the northwest.

Kelsey spotted it from a high rim where, with Teal and Running Wolf, he had ridden ahead for a look at the forward country. A quick concern rose in him when he looked down upon the strung-out wagons with their long double files of yoked oxen heeling hard against earth already softened by the rains of early fall.

Ever since the Big Hole, when they had been betrayed by the settlers they had trusted, the Nez Percés had looked upon all white men as enemies and all property in line with their own needs as legitimate prizes of war. Here was a chance to replenish supplies, relieving the growing and dangerous desire among the Indians to halt and hunt for buffalo.

He said, "Going to be trouble. There's more stuff on them wagons than Halverson could have packed here in a month of Sundays."

Teal nodded. "Every time something like this happens, I make myself think of my helpless sister burned to death in her bed and my mother shot through the head and my cousin's baby with its hand shot off. Then I can stand what has to happen if we are to live at all."

Without speaking, Running Wolf swung his pony and rode off. Kelsey knew he was going to report the discovery, that a party of warriors would be here presently. He said, "You go with him, Teal."

"Where are you going?"

"To give those poor devils a chance to save themselves."

"All right."

He had to follow the rim for some distance, hunting

a way to descend. When he looked back, both Teal and Running Wolf had vanished. He had gone on only a short way when abruptly he pulled down his horse, rising on his stirrup leathers and staring down into the coulee that broke ahead of him. Horsemen that he estimated at around forty were plodding forward on a course that would intercept the freight train.

Militia company, he thought bleakly, out of Benton.

For an instant panic all but wheeled him about to carry a warning to the Indians. The situation was simple enough to explain itself to him. The militia must have realized that the freight train was in this vicinity, probably having picked up its load from the steamboat that had recently been at Cow Island. It was obvious that the wagons would be overtaken by the Indians and attacked. This company planned to let that happen and strike at that point in surprise.

Swinging his horse about, he began to retrace his course along the bench. Long before he could make up his mind what to do, he could see the Nez Percé war party whip into view on the bottom below, coming around the distant point in a silent, rushing mass. He estimated its number at around twenty, less than half that of the volunteers.

Far to the left the wagons came to a sudden halt. Kelsey saw a puff of smoke and then another before the first dulled cracks of rifle shots reached his ears. But the warriors swept on, their own rifles answering.

Without any estimate of how many men were in the freighter party, Kelsey felt admiration for their reckless courage. They put up a bristling defense of their wagons, against which the warriors rode without faltering, hanging low on their ponies as they began to circle in. Oddly and against what a man would expect, the militia did not put in an appearance. He saw oxen collapse and settle to the earth and he saw warriors flung from their racing ponies. The recent rains kept down the dust so that the grim details were all too vivid.

Still the hidden force of volunteers held back, sitting their horses while white and red men took lead and died. Presently the dwindling shooting died out, and warriors were swarming over the wagons. He could see wagon sheets ripped open and some of the wagon contents being thrown to the ground. Then came the first rise of smoke as the wagons and remaining freight were set afire. Rising to horse, the Indians wheeled off to bring in pack ponies to pick up the chosen supplies.

Then and only then did the militia appear, spilling out of the western obscurity of rock and land swells. Why they had waited so long would forever remain a mystery to Kelsey. The Nez Percés fired back as they kept riding. The militia pursued them only for a short distance and then pulled off. At last Kelsey swung his horse away, riding slowly. A little later he came to a place where he could see the volunteer detachment riding swiftly southward toward the Missouri, pulling out.

CHAPTER EIGHTEEN

Two days north of the Bear's Paw Mountains there came a cold and slashing rain that was snow at the higher elevations. But the border was now only forty miles away, a distance that one forced march could cover. Because he had not himself suffered the long attrition that had worn bare the very souls of the Nez Percés, Kelsey could sense the nervous and physical exhaustion that was overwhelming them just short of that sanctuary.

He knew that there was quarreling among the chiefs, a rising demand in the people for rest and above all for the fresh meat so long denied their punished bodies. The only force that had come against them since far-off Canyon Creek, they argued, had fired only a few timid shots and then pulled out. This was the last chance to make meat in good buffalo country, and there was a rear guard to warn them if anything menacing appeared on the long trail from the Missouri.

So camp was set up on Snake Creek where it ran through encircling bluffs that fended off the cold wind and gave sweeping vistas of the rearward country. No tree stood within the eye's reach and no human habitation rose within many miles.

Kelsey rose in a raw dawn, thinking of his plans to go with Teal's brothers on a private hunt. But between breakfast and the saddling of his horse a warrior came with word that Halverson insisted on seeing him and Teal.

They found Halverson standing before a tepee. Without preamble, he said, "Look. Are they going to keep me here indefinitely while they hunt their damned buffalo?"

"Looks that way, doesn't it?" Kelsey said.

"I think you two could talk them into letting me go, if you wanted to. Hell, Ames, we've had our differences but why can't you help a man out?"

"You can dish it out better than you can take it, huh?"

"Damn it, man, I don't have time to waste this way. I've got a business to run. I don't know what harm they think I could do them. Why don't you see Joseph and put in a word for me?"

"The main reason," Kelsey said, "is that I don't mind a bit seeing you sweat. And if that's all you wanted to see us about, it's tended to. Come on, Teal."

"Ames," Halverson said desperately, "I'll make it right with you."

Swinging about, Kelsey gave him a long, flat stare. "Only one way to do that. Die as hard as the people whose deaths you've caused. That would make it right with me, Halverson, and I hope to see it."

He left with Teal then, a little shaken by the raw fear he had glimpsed deep in the mind of the man. It rose from echoes in Halverson himself, reminders of too many debts too long unpaid. . . .

The pony herd grazed on the bunch grass about the camp. With Ten Owl and Running Wolf, Kelsey rode past, staring at a forecountry of continuing plateau dotted only by prickly pear and sage. A sense of serenity began to build in him, a feeling that Joseph had won his freedom and the freedom of his people. He knew that runners had already been sent to find Sitting Bull and inform him of the Nez Percés' approach. There was at least an even chance that the rebellious Sioux would come with help in case there was yet an attack.

With the light scarcely brightened in the day's full strength, they bent their course in against the northern arm of the mountains, climbing eventually onto its slope for a better look at the prairie. It surprised Kelsey that, while he and his companions could hold no conversation whatsoever, they were able to communicate quite well in matters of necessity. And it was all too intelligible when Running Wolf presently let out a sound of pure dismay and stared hard at the mountain slope above him. Kelsey followed suit when the Indians quickly cut their ponies back into cover.

He had seen nothing up there but the unbroken line where brown earth cut against the leaden sky. The two Indians exchanged low, terse talk, then Running Wolf held rounded fingers to his eyes and followed that by using a hand to describe a feathered headdress, and Kelsey understood. They had detected a spying Indian.

Running Wolf now gestured toward the camp, and Kelsey nodded. He pointed at himself and then the higher slope of the mountain, for he intended to scout the situation while they returned to warn the camp. He was not greatly concerned as yet; a spying Indian could mean anything or nothing. The Indians whipped their ponies into a draw and then were lost to view.

He rode back for some distance on the tracks of his brothers-in-law, then swung left and began to climb the slope along the bottom of a low saddle. He allowed himself a considerable distance before he began to bend eastward, alert and forced to assume that his presence was known to the spying Indian or Indians. When finally he dared to top out, it was to gaze upon a scene that to him was horror.

There swept forward below him on a broad, trotting front an enormous force of cavalry regulars. He all but cried out his protest and, frozen, sat his saddle in hypnotic attention. Over three hundred horses drummed the prairie with an increasing cadence. It was unbelievable, a nightmare trick of the senses in a place where it was wholly impossible. But the command was bending inexorably on the head of Snake Creek, which would take it in upon the Indian encampment. That was real—too real to contemplate.

It dawned upon him finally that there was a far graver situation here than Running Wolf and Ten Owl would report to the camp. He swung his horse about, only to find himself staring at the pointed rifles of two mounted Indians who were stripped for action. They were Cheyennes, hardy scouts of the Seventh Cavalry, a breed of men he had once admired. Now they stared at him in steady, deeply suspicious hostility.

Rebellion ran through him. He could not submit to capture with what he knew to be bearing down upon Teal as well as all her people, and his hand streaked for the grips of his gun. He got hold of it, but that was the last he knew. Something caved in his world. . . .

He regained his senses to the cracking of massed rifles. He could detect the heavier punching of Gatling guns and cannon. He knew that the Army had at last brought up the full force of its wrath. He got his eyes open and found himself lying in a dry wash. Sage fringed the tops of the bank so that there was revealed to him only a patch of glowering sky.

A voice said, "Easy, buck. You had a close call."

He looked about to see a trooper watching him from a seat on the sandy ground, and the same glance revealed that there were other hurt men stretched about. It dawned on him that he had been brought in to the field hospital, that the fight was well under way. He managed to sit up and return the orderly's bald stare.

"Maybe it'll be a lesson to you," the trooper said. "Don't ever let yourself give the impression of spying on an Army movement. One of our scouts nearly blew off your fool head."

"Impression? Goddamn you, man, I *was* spying. My wife's with the Indians. Why in hell can't you leave them alone?"

"That's a good question, buck, and more than one asked it of hisself when we come in. The Fifth and Seventh led the parade, and pretty it was to see. But them blasted redskins just stood up and poured it back. Then it wasn't pretty any more. When that charge wheeled back, half of the mounts wore empty saddles."

"Damn it, my wife—"

"Take it easy. Maybe she's all right. Some of the

families got away and went north hell ahiking."

Kelsey subsided then, shaking his head again and again. He said, "How in the devil did you get across the river?"

"Steamboat. Miles caught the Benton and made it ferry us over."

And there it was, the improbability that now was a dead certainty, the chance in a hundred come up and spelling doom. "Am I a prisoner?"

"Not that I know of. But I'd sure keep my head down. This thing ain't the pushover they told us it would be."

His head throbbed with crashing, pulsing pain, and had been bandaged, he discovered. Once again he had escaped death only because of a hasty shot that had gone astray of its mark. The bullet of the Cheyenne scout had split his scalp at the part of the hair, its impact having put him out of it as swiftly as death itself. He still could think only with sluggish patience, and he picked at what he had learned and kept trying to believe that Teal had been with the Nez Percé women who had got clear of it. But he doubted that. It was not in her nature to run when her people were in danger.

The crash of the battle never diminished. More wounded slipped into the coulee to receive the hospital orderly's services and more were carried in. Kelsey heard a man saying bitterly, "God, did we catch a bear by the tail! I heard Erickson tell Miles he was the only damned officer of the Seventh left alive. Every time I been in an Indian fight, it's been this way. We go in with our tails up and we come out with 'em shot off. Six hundred men we got, and the scouts say there's hardly a hundred warriors. And damn if we ain't the ones fighting for our lives already."

Kelsey pushed himself up, staring hard at the speaker. He gasped, "Six hundred? Have more come in?"

The man gave him a quick, hard stare. "Who're you, anyhow?"

"A year ago I was Sergeant Ames of the Seventh, son. Maybe about the time you were getting the green ground off of you at Lincoln. Let it go at that."

"That a fact?" the orderly said in surprise.

"And right now not a bit proud of it, friend."

"He's got a woman with the redskins," the orderly explained to the newcomer, whose arm he was dressing.

"Not a woman, mister. My wife."

"All right, all right."

Shaking his hurting head, Kelsey let his temper subside. These men were not to blame for what was happening here. Orders had brought them and orders now held them here, hurt, frightened, and as bewildered as himself. Lying there and listening, he learned that the Indians had been forced into the coulees, from which they now returned a hot retort. A battalion of Second Cavalry had swung in on the rear to cut off escape and to separate the Nez Percés from the pony herd. The animals had been captured and moved away. Meanwhile a troop had gone in pursuit of the Indians who had got away.

Kelsey heard that last in bitter despair. But he could only lie weakly, listening to the wrathful rifles and waiting for nightfall. After it came, he would try to reach Teal and share whatever was left for her to experience. Yet from the position of the sun, he knew that darkness was yet an eternity away; as remote as the border that for so long had meant sanctuary. . . .

A little before one o'clock word seeped into the hospital coulee that Colonel Miles had ordered another charge, a mass maneuver involving his entire force. Also, it was rumored, he had sent word to General Howard to hurry his own huge force forward. Almost before that was digested, the mounting fury of guns was heard. Kelsey at last rose to a crouch, unable to bear inaction a second longer, and he found his legs grown steadier. He moved to the top of the slope, ignoring the warnings.

Sagebrush gave him a degree of concealment there, and he found that they were on the extreme southwest edge of the battlefield, in no direct line of fire. Behind this position rose one of the several hummocks in the vicinity, unoccupied and also smothered in rank sage. Again the hospital orderly spoke an uneasy objection. Paying no attention, Kelsey crawled on.

He gained his objective without difficulty, finding himself on an elevation that showed him the entire battlefield. Many of the tepees of the village were down, and he could see none of the Indians from where he lay.

From what he had learned of the disposition of the forces, he was quickly able to get his bearings. On the bluffs across from him, remnants of the shot-up Seventh and Second Cavalry had pressed down and were now engaged in a desperate struggle on the lower slopes and draws. To his right and above Snake Creek, the Fifth Infantry was likewise bringing in an attack, flattened and crawling in upon the village. Retaliatory shooting showed him, finally, that the Nez Percé fighters were on the bluffs to the south and in the sloughs directly below them. The women, the children, the old ones—only God knew where they were, and how could a man believe that He cared?

Yet the defense firing was too heavy for the troops to carry out their objectives. Only once in the next two hours of steady, unrelenting shooting was there a sign of a change in the deadly and deadlocked pattern.

What appeared to be two squads of the Fifth Infantry broke recklessly down the slope and succeeded in reaching the village, which they apparently were intent upon firing. But Indians rose from somewhere, and a fierce hand-to-hand struggle followed. Kelsey saw at least five soldiers go down, the rest running for nearby draws and gullies. Then, around three o'clock, the attackers began to draw back. Miles had learned his lesson, Kelsey reflected. He was not going to be able to overrun the camp without a fearful cost in lives. The trudging Howard apparently was not far distant. The wiser interim action would be a siege.

The fighting diminished, although the firing continued steadily. Now Kelsey was able to take note of the darkening skies, no harbinger of dusk, and of the brisk wind and its cutting coldness. Thirst began to gnaw at him as he patiently awaited his chance to get through to his wife. Finally he crawled down to the creek, which skirted his position, and drank. Afterward he rested, hidden in the sage, oddly burning from what he feared was a growing fever, yet chilled by the biting wind.

Afterward he drowsed, and when he awakened it was to feel the cold impact of a snowflake upon his face.

CHAPTER NINETEEN

HE was never afterward sure of how he worked his way through the lines. Past nightfall and in a whipping snow, he simply began to move toward his objective, which was Teal, who was his wife and without whom he was as dead as the hundred men whose life threads had that day been snapped.

Somehow he crossed the wind-swept open and got into the dry wash that snaked through the Indian camp, knowing that all about him others crawled desperately, soldiers cut off and trying to get back to their outfits, Nez Percés trying to make contact with their fellows.

He came first upon a group of women and children flattened in shelter pits they had dug with their hands. The wash was full of noncombatants, and he pressed on, speaking Teal's name to all he saw. At last a boy who shivered in buckskin leggings caught his hand and began to draw him to the left.

She saw him first, a low cry coming to him out of a group flattened on the snow-dusted ground.

"Kelsey! Oh, Kelsey!"

When he had dropped beside her, he could do nothing but flatten a hand on her shoulder and feel her trembling, feel her own hand so carefully explore him to answer unvoiced and terrible questions.

She whispered, "My brothers were certain the Cheyennes had killed you."

"Not quite. Are they all right?"

"I don t know."

She was crying then, clinging to him.

The battle lessened as the night deepened, but the fall of snow grew heavier, the wind more insistently chilling. The people had fled their lodges so hastily that there had been no time to catch up blankets, spare clothing, or food. Because of the siege lines about the camp, there could be no fires for warmth.

Huddled with Teal, he learned from her that the day's fighting had cost the lives of three of the chiefs: Looking Glass of her old village; Ollicott, the young and handsome; and Tuhulhutsut, the old medicine man. There was only one hope left, help from Sitting Bull, if the Nez Percés could hold out until he came with his fearless Sioux. Runners had slipped out to make contact with him.

Kelsey felt an anger that was not of the mind, now, but of the heart itself. There was much that he could do, for in the lessened fighting the Nez Percés were stubbornly digging in. On the bluffs and open slopes, Indians used knives or their bare hands to dig rifle pits for the warriors and shelter pits for the rest. There were wounded everywhere to be attended and dead to be buried. There was never enough water, which had to be brought in driblets from near the enemy lines. But he helped, with everything he had in him and in spite of the pain and sickness that racked his own body.

He had forgotten Lafe Halverson until he stumbled onto the man in the coulee where he was held.

"Ames! By God, I'm glad to see you, man!"

"You've got it over me, then."

"You've got to help me get through to the Army lines!"

"I hope you get one of their slugs through your belly, damn you. This is the sort of thing you've been working for. Don't expect any sympathy from me."

"By God, Ames, you're not human!"

The laugh from Kelsey's throat was not pleasant.

Morning came with the warriors better entrenched than they had been the day before. Light was a brand touched to the fuses in every gun. The upper air was wild and roiling; at earth level it was a blasting, snow-thickened wind. At first dawn Kelsey seized up a rifle some lifeless hand had dropped and moved into the firing line. His lips pinched as he heard the resumed coughing of the howitzer that sent its destroying charges directly in upon the shelter pits.

He got his first target sooner than he had expected, a blue-clad figure on the downslope directly across from him. Yet someplace between brain and trigger finger, his reaction died in him. The man over there was cold and hungry and fearful for his life. Then, when something caused him to look back over his shoulder, he saw Teal crawling toward him.

When she came up, she lay for a moment panting. Then, scarcely able to whisper, she said, "There's got to be warm food! At least for the wounded and children! If you'll help me, I'm going to build a fire in the wash."

"You'll draw a shell from the howitzer."

"I don't care."

He returned with her, crawling back into the slough under the firing heights. Running Wolf and some others, she told him, had brought in horse flesh. She wanted to make a hot soup, and if Kelsey could gather enough buffalo chips for her, she would risk the smoke of a fire. He took one look into the depths of her eyes and agreed to try it.

It was considerable of an undertaking, he realized as he set about it. The whole prairie now lay under a blanket of snow, even if he could get out there safely and return alive. He got a sack, then followed the dry wash westward, convinced that Miles would not have left it uncovered. But he was not challenged, and this discovery started a faint hope in his mind.

When he was far enough into the prairie for ground swells to hide him, he began his patient hunt for buffalo chips. He had to locate them by feel of foot, then dig them out with freezing fingers. It seemed forever before he had filled the sack, and then he started in to the entrapment again.

Teal was more pleased with his offering than if it had been a bag of jewels. Together with some other women, she had gone to the deepest part of the wash and there scraped back the snow. Without kindling, he had trouble starting a fire of the punklike fuel, but when finally it was burning he was relieved to see that its faint smoke was quickly frayed by the wind and lost in the swirling snowflakes. There were large, bloody chunks of meat carved from some shot horse, and the women prepared the reed baskets in which they cooked with hot stones.

He said, "Teal, I got in and out without any trouble. Either they haven't noticed that the wash runs out the way it does or else somebody who's supposed to guard it figured it was just too cold."

She looked up at him quickly. "You mean you think we could slip away?"

"Hard to see far in this snow. I figured maybe you'd want to tell Joseph. They've been too busy fighting to scout around."

"I will," she said promptly, and rose from the fire.

She was not gone long. When she came back to him she shook her head. "He says it would mean leaving our sick and wounded, and he won't do that. He says he has never heard of a hurt Indian recovering in the hands of white men."

"He still hopes Sitting Bull will come and relieve us?"

"When hope dies, then so does the spirit, and the whole person is better dead."

And he knew that that faint ray of hope, seen through the swirling flakes of snow, was all that sustained the Nez Percés through that bitter day of fighting. Miles now was content with his siege, and his sure knowledge that Howard's big force was not far away. So from the bluffs about rifles poured their deadliness in upon the Indians, the Gatling guns sporadically spewing, the howitzer delivering its disastrous cannonade.

All day women and children died with the warriors; all day numbed flesh weakened in the unrelenting attrition. In afternoon the snowfall dwindled, then quit, and in early evening Miles's big wagon train of supplies pulled in to rest in the safe ground saddle where the regulars had their hospital.

"They've got everything!" Teal moaned, and Kelsey knew she was thinking of the horse meat that had not been nearly enough to feed her people.

"Ah, no," he said. "They don't have everything."

A wildly reckless urge was rising in him. On that train were food, medicines, blankets, spare clothing. Along the wash and in the sloughs were shot warriors, sick children and women and old ones. Up on the bluffs were more who were hurt or sick but still fighting grimly. He would give anything he had, including his life, for one roll of bandage, one can of quinine, one blanket.

No Indian could live long enough to reach such supplies, but maybe a white man could. Considering it carefully, he thought suddenly of another white man and had his plan. Quietly he made his way to where Lafe Halverson lay shivering on the ground.

He said, "Soon as it's dark enough, we'll try to get through the lines."

Halverson sat up quickly. "You mean it? But what

changed your mind?"

"You can help me."

"I'll do anything to get out of this."

"All right. You're going to help me raid their hospital of things they can replace easily now that their supply train's come up. You owe your life to these people. If you'll help me. I'll let you stay over there."

"I will—I will!"

Seeking Teal, Kelsey told her of his plan and had her arrange for Halverson's release to him. There were rifles and pistols aplenty now, more than there were hands to fire them. He armed himself with an Army pistol picked up on some past battleground. Only three shells remained in its cylinder, but that did not matter. He wanted the gun only for its persuasive power.

It was dark enough to start by then. Ushering the eager Halverson along the wash he had followed out after buffalo chips, he moved out onto the snow-carpeted prairie.

He said, "We're going to try to get on the hill west of the train. The hospital's just below it. I know the setup. There'll be an orderly or so, maybe a surgeon, and by now a raft of wounded. We're going to slip in, and while I hold this gun on them you're going to make me up a pack of all I can carry back. If I have to shoot anybody at all, it'll be you, man. Don't you forget that."

He could make out the shape of the hummock that was their objective and from this position could see lights that were cut from view of the Indians by the bluff. Miles, he realized, had set up headquarters in that sheltered canyon, had settled in comparative comfort to the task at hand.

Kelsey led Halverson farther onto the prairie until they came to a shallow trough that let them cross the creek and brought them in finally on the western slope of the hummock. They immediately crossed over to the other side and were within easy shouting distance of the opaque headquarters tents. If Halverson had any thought of treachery at that point, his fear of Kelsey's gun and grim threat put it down.

There was lantern light in the hospital coulee, where badly injured men had to be given attention regardless of the night. Kelsey nudged Halverson, who moved that way with a step suddenly turned reluctant. They crawled the last distance, snow caught in the heavy sagebrush spilling upon them. Then Kelsey found himself looking down upon a testimonial to Indian marksmanship far greater than he had anticipated. He could not see all of the coulee, but within his range of vision there must have been the pallets of forty or fifty wounded men.

He whispered, "All right," to Halverson, then they rose and started openly down the last descending distance. An officer with the bars of a captain was bent over a litter, a corporal helping him. Neither looked up at the scuff of steps in the snow.

"Easy," Kelsey said quietly. "I've got a gun on you. All we want is some stuff for people as bad off as yours, Doc—stuff you can replace from the wagons."

The surgeon, binding a wounded leg, flung up a quick, shocked stare. His orderly breathed, "By God, it's that squaw man we had here!"

The surgeon watched Kelsey through baffled eyes. His face was lined with fatigue under a graying beard. He said, "I remember dressing his wound. And farther back than that, I think. Didn't I give you your physical when you were mustered out at Fort Lincoln, son?"

"That you did, sir."

"You've changed since then."

"Ah, yes."

"And turned traitor!" Halverson all but yelled. "I let him think I'd help him with this, but I won't! They've held me a prisoner nearly a week, officer! Go ahead and use that gun, Ames. You all but admitted you don't have the stomach to do it."

"Damn your black soul to hell," Kelsey said softly, and knew that from the beginning Halverson had recognized that weakness and had used it cynically.

"Arrest him, somebody!" Halverson shouted.

The officer said, "Put away the gun, Ames. Corporal, make him up what he wants and, let him have it."

"You bet," the corporal said, and he sounded pleased.

"You're not going to let him get away with this!" Halverson spluttered.

"Personally, I wish I could go and help them myself."

Lacking a holster, Kelsey shoved the pistol into the band of his pants. There was a glint in his eyes as he watched the surgeon and his assistant make quick selections of medicines and bandages and make them into a blanket pack. Halverson stood bewildered. Then he swung and, half running, headed for the distant headquarters tent.

"I expect you'd better hurry," the surgeon said as the corporal handed Kelsey the pack.

"Sir, I thank you from my heart."

"Luck to you and yours."

Kelsey melted into the darkness, even less sure than the doctor of the impression Halverson would make at headquarters. From the elevation he looked back, but the tents had swallowed Halverson. It galled him to the core to have the man free. But he had been obliged to make the play for his help. He could not have known that he was going to put a gun on a man worthy of the bars he wore.

Somewhere between that point and the Indian position he began to realize the toll taken of him. The fever that had smoldered since he had been shot seemed suddenly to burst into full flame. Twice he fell sprawling in the snow but each time pushed up and went on.

Since Teal was the only one in all that throng with whom he could talk, he again sought her to make the best distribution she could of what he had received from the Army surgeon. But he never found her. Barely within the Indian lines, he went flat in the snow and could not get up again. A crushing drowsiness held him, and at last he gave in to its urging.

When he awakened it was daylight and the burning fever seemed to have left him. He was lying on a buffalo robe with something piled on top, a discovery that shamed him instantly. He pushed up, dizzy and still bone-weary, and found himself with a large, huddled group of women and children in the shelter pits. One of them called out, and then he saw Teal running toward him.

"What happened?" he gasped. "They're not shooting."

She shook her head but still wore a look of deep concern. "A messenger came under a flag of truce saying Colonel Miles wanted to talk it over with Joseph. Joseph went and he hasn't come back. Yellow Bull's in command, and he thinks they've taken Joseph prisoner to force us to surrender."

"The dirty sons!" Kelsey exploded. "I see Lafe Halverson's hand in that! He told them how miserably hopeless it is over here. I ought to have shot him in cold blood. But I couldn't kill any man that way." She looked puzzled, so he told her of how Halverson had broken the promise he had made and about the surgeon's unexpected humaneness.

"I'm glad you didn't kill him," she said. "I think there are higher forces that tend to such matters in the end. We oughtn't to take them into our own hands unless we have to. My darling, I'm so grateful for what you did."

"It's hopeless, honey."

"I know. But people can be glorious even in despair, and these are. Would you leave them now, even if I'd come with you?"

"No."

"And that, my man, is why I so very dearly love you."

CHAPTER TWENTY

T HE day passed in uneasy truce. Joseph did not return from the Army camp, and as the hours stretched out, Indian nerves and patience stretched with them, heightening the conviction that once again he had met with deceit and treachery.

Bitterly Kelsey said to Teal, "Every time the government makes overtures to the Indians, it wheedles and promises, then turns right around and does some damned thing to show it can't be trusted. I used to figure we got a fine country, and I still think so. But God save us from some of the people who handle its business."

Late in the morning warriors caught an Army lieutenant trying to reconnoiter the camp and took him into custody. Yellow Bull thereupon crossed the lines boldly, going directly to Miles's headquarters, where he threatened to kill the officer if Joseph was harmed. Yellow Bull was allowed to return, but still Joseph was not released.

The prolonged absence of their leader had a depressing effect on the Indians, and Kelsey supposed that was what Miles hoped to accomplish. The night passed restlessly. Then, in the morning, another messenger came in under a truce flag with an offer to exchange the two prisoners. The offer was accepted promptly.

Kelsey watched the exchange, which took place midway between the two camps. Accompanied by several officers, Chief Joseph came across the snow to the halfway point, which had been marked by a buffalo robe. He knew that more than one hidden, distrustful Indian rifle covered the group, for who could believe the people of the forked tongues? The officers out there seemed to realize that. As the Indians came up with their own prisoner, the officers offered their hands. The trade was made briskly, and each party returned to its own side.

Joseph addressed his people immediately. He had, he said, been treated like a common criminal and not as the chief of a people whose limited autonomy the government had many times promised to respect. He had been bound and kept under guard with the Army mules. It showed, Teal reported him as saying, what they could expect if they surrendered. The war had to continue.

His outrage leaped to the listeners and brought forth a resounding roar. Again blood was hot, although the relentless wind could freeze the flesh. In the far-off Wallowa, on the Clearwater, in the valley of the Bitterroot—always there had been honeyed words and bitter deeds.

So again warriors squirmed in the rifle pits and behind their small forts of piled rock, subject to wind and snow and probing lead. Across the field the mountain howitzer resumed its efforts, searching the shelter pits, seeking still and shivering flesh. It was the fifth morning of fighting.

Then, near noon, a shell made a direct hit on a shelter pit, burying four women, a small boy, and a half-grown girl in the dirt and snow of the bank. Only two women and the girl were alive when they were dug out.

It seemed an eternity spent in hell itself before darkness again settled in. In the darkness an Indian with frozen hands and feet crawled up the wash. His appearance sent a great electric impulse across the encampment, for he was one of the runners dispatched to Sitting Bull.

He could not talk immediately. Kelsey had come up with Teal to join the prayerful press about when finally he could speak to Joseph. He had not reached the camp of Sitting Bull, he said, for the camp was gone from where it had been. He had learned from an Assiniboin that the Sioux chief had heard of the fighting here and had promptly pulled deeper into the country of the redcoats to escape being drawn into this new trouble.

"There was never any help or hope of it," Teal whispered. "From the Crows, the Sioux, or from God Himself," and his hand upon her shoulder felt a low and terrible laugh.

After telling the listeners to disperse, Joseph went into council with his remaining chiefs. It was quickly over, the leaders dissolving among the people. Shortly afterward Running Wolf and Ten Owl sought Teal. Kelsey could not understand what passed between them but he could all too plainly recognize a cry of protest from her. Then he saw in the darkness the reluctant assent of her head.

"They're going," she said, turning to Kelsey. "White

Bird is taking the younger people who want to go in an effort to reach the border, anyway. Joseph wants it so. He says that this is not in vain if somewhere there are Nez Percés living as free men and women."

"You want to go, Teal?" he asked.

"My brothers say my place is with you, and they are right."

Kelsey could only hold out his hand to the men and feel their strong grips and watch them dissolve forever into the stormy night.

"And the rest?" he said to Teal.

"They will fight on to the end."

That was a thought too ghastly, too mocking for him to contemplate. But he was entirely helpless as well as devoid of any desire to urge her to leave with him now that the end had come. There was no increase in the shooting from the Army lines, indicating that White Bird was successfully slipping his people out of the encircled camp. Then cold and apathy again prevailed.

It was shortly after daylight when an Indian woman crawled up to where Kelsey lay with Teal, their close-pressed bodies their only source of warmth. When she heard the woman's low talk, Teal said, "An officer has slipped over from the other side, Kelsey. He wants to talk to you."

Kelsey followed the woman down the wash and presently saw the figure of a captain seated on the bank.

"Captain Drummond of the Seventh," the officer said, as Kelsey came up. "Possibly you remember me."

"That I do, Surgeon. But why are you here?"

"The Colonel asked me to talk to you. He thought maybe you could persuade Joseph to stop this slaughter."

"Joseph stop it? It's a bad time to joke, Captain."

"Ah," the surgeon said. "If only it were a joke! But Howard came up last night. There's absolutely no chance that more fighting could end in anything but more tragedy. That's what Miles wanted you to tell the Chief. Coming from a friend, it might persuade him."

"And what does the Colonel offer?"

"To feed and clothe these people and give them medical treatment. To take them to a good place to winter and return them to their homeland in the spring."

"On a reservation?"

"I'm afraid so, Ames."

"I'll relay no promises that I don't think will be kept."

"I don't blame you for being bitter. But you know general orders: Pursue the enemy and destroy him. Miles, Sturgis, Gibbons, Howard—no commander who's come against the Nez Percés could have done other than what he did. You know that, Ames."

"I guess."

"The Colonel," Drummond continued, "is an astute man and fairer than you suppose. It might interest you to know that Lafe Halverson is now under military arrest."

"How come?" Kelsey asked, astonished.

"On Joseph's account of what Halverson was doing

up here, as against Halverson's own story. His insistence that Halverson offered to back a general uprising ties in with too many other things already known about the man. And another thing that pertains to you, Ames."

"So?"

"Joseph gave you a clean bill of health. Personally, you're in no trouble. Actually, I think the Colonel would like to shake your hand."

"I don't give a damn about me, Captain. It's these people. They've come a long way and they've had nothing but heartbreak and treachery and disloyalty, straight down the line. Something fine came out of them, and what they do now must come out of them, too. I won't encourage Joseph or the smallest tyke in the band to surrender because you think they're licked. They're not, and you don't have enough army to whip them any time or anywhere."

Drummond stood. "All right, Ames. The Colonel will have to issue an ultimatum. Surrender—or else." He offered his hand.

Yet it was close to noon before Miles took any further action. Then suddenly two Indians appeared on the other side, carrying a flag of truce. They were not Cheyennes, but Nez Percés, treaty Indians from far-off Idaho, men who had scouted for Howard from the beginning. Their appearance had a cogency that cut through the watchers like a knife, for it announced beyond dispute that Howard had caught up at last. It was a crushing blow, and Kelsey saw the last feeble faith die out of many faces.

One of the emissaries called something that Teal interpreted swiftly.

"All my brothers! I am glad to see you alive, this sun!"

They came on, and some of the watchers shifted their weapons. But a subchief gave a low warning and the hostility subsided. Then the messengers were hurried off to where Joseph rested.

"You knew?" Teal said, searching Kelsey's face.

"Yes. They wanted me to be the one to tell Joseph, but I wouldn't."

"More fighting would be suicide," she said brokenly. "But the people will do it if Joseph tells them to."

Yet Joseph quickly sent the emissaries back to their own lines. Then another council was held. Waiting for the outcome, Teal said, "What will we do if he surrenders?"

"He already cleared me with the Army. Must have been in that first powwow with the Colonel. I'd be free to go, I reckon, and you'd be free as my wife. Would you?"

"It is as my brothers told me. My place is with you."

It seemed that another two hours passed before Miles's Indian representatives again came across the open ground. Everyone who watched knew that they were coming for Joseph's decision. This time, instead of receiving them privately, Joseph appeared before all the people who remained to him. Watching, Kelsey felt something stir at a depth he had not known he possessed.

"When hope dies, then so does the spirit," Teal once

said, and here was a man already dead upon his feet. Joseph spoke slowly, between heavy drags of breath, and in each pause Teal whispered the words to her husband.

"I am tired of fighting. Our chiefs are killed. Looking Glass is dead. Tuhulhutsut is dead. The old men are all dead. It is the young men who say yes or no. He who led the young men is dead.

"It is cold and we have no blankets. The little children are freezing to death. My people, some of them, have run away to the hills and have no blankets, no food. No one knows where they are—perhaps freezing to death.

"I want to have time to look for my children and see how many of them I can find. Maybe I shall find them among the dead.

"Hear me, my chiefs. I am tired. My heart is sick and sad. From where the sun now stands I will fight no more forever."

His head tipped forward, and he was that way as the scouts turned to carry his decision to the victors.

Center Point Publishing
600 Brooks Road • PO Box 1
Thorndike ME 04986-0001 USA

(207) 568-3717

US & Canada:
1 800 929-9108